KOKOPELLI'S FLUTE

Other Books by
Will Hobbs

BEARDANCE
BEARSTONE
THE BIG WANDER
CHANGES IN LATITUDES
FAR NORTH
GHOST CANOE
JASON'S GOLD
THE MAZE

WILL HOBBS has long been intrigued by the ancient pueblo people of the Southwest and the remarkable cliff dwellings they left behind in the Four Corners area of Colorado, Utah, Arizona, and New Mexico. From their home near Durango, Colorado, Will and his wife, Jean, have backpacked into remote canyons to visit ruins like the one in KOKOPELLI'S FLUTE. To find out more about Will Hobbs, visit his website at **www.WillHobbsAuthor.com**

KOKOPELLI'S FLUTE

WILL HOBBS

AN AVON  CAMELOT BOOK

AVON BOOKS, INC.
1350 Avenue of the Americas
New York, New York 10019

Copyright © 1995 by Will Hobbs
Published by arrangement with Simon & Schuster
Library of Congress Catalog Card Number: 95-8422
ISBN: 0-380-72818-4
RL: 5.8
www.avonbooks.com

First Avon Camelot Printing: May 1997

CAMELOT TRADEMARK REG. U.S. PAT OFF. AND IN OTHER COUNTRIES, MARCA REGISTRADA,
HECHO EN U S.A

Printed in the U.S.A.

For my sister Barbara

with special thanks to Dusty for Dusty

Chapter One

The magic had always been there. In the light, in the rock, in the miniature city the Ancient Ones left perched in the cliffs. I've always felt it. It seems like every day of my life I've been trying to get a little closer to the magic. This would be the night I not only got close, but crossed over.

The long June day was ending as I was hiking to the ruin with my dog, Dusty. This was going to be my first total eclipse of the moon, and I wanted to witness it from Picture House. For all the time I'd spent there, puzzling over the secrets of the ancient pueblo, I've never had an opportunity like a total eclipse. Maybe during the eclipse, if I listened hard enough, I might hear the footsteps of the Ancient Ones. I might even hear their voices. It might be a matter of being in the right place at the right time. Who knows, I might even see dancers appearing on the dance plaza from their underground kivas.

After the eclipse, I'd have my night-hike back home. Night is my favorite time, and every so often I hike by the moon. Like Ringo, my pet ringtail, I was born nocturnal. All the sleep I've ever needed is a few winks here and there. Tepary Jones is my name, after the fabulous tepary bean, of course.

Dusty and I stopped at the spring where the people from Picture House had come for centuries to get their water. Despite how dry it had been this year, water was still gushing from a thin layer of shale and falling into the pool below. The cliffs and the mesa tops were glowing with the last reflections of the sunset as we watched the full moon rise over the canyon rims of our out-of-the-way corner of northern New Mexico.

I shucked my clothes and dove into the pool. A cool jolt ran through me like electricity. "Jump in, girl!" I called to Dusty, and she did. I'm thirteen, and Dusty just turned eleven. At her age, even a natural swimmer like a golden retriever takes a little bit of encouragement, but there's a lot of puppy left in that old dog's heart.

I climbed out and shivered, and Dusty shook, and I rested my back against the slab jutting twenty feet into the air. A minute later I was dry and comfortable. The slab is an ancient creek bed turned to stone. You can

2

still see the wavy water lines that the receding creek left behind, and even the tracks of a turkey-sized dinosaur that walked across the mud and left its mark in time.

Still a couple of hours until the eclipse. I dressed, and we threaded our way through the scrubby pinyon pines and junipers we call a forest around here, until we could see Picture House with its five kivas, forty-three rooms, and two towers gleaming across the ancient dance plaza. The cave that housed the cliff dwelling soared high and wide, dished out of the arching cliff. Eight hundred years ago the people came through all those little doorways for the last time, walked away, and left only stiffness, silence, and secrets.

This is where I wanted to watch, to try to feel what the people must have felt when they witnessed an eclipse of the moon from Picture House. I curled up a stone's throw from the ruin and started snacking on a bag of pinyon nuts. Sitting on her haunches, Dusty's face was on a level with mine. Her muzzle was grizzled these days, like she'd stuck it in a bag of flour. I pointed at the moon, so close it seemed you could reach out and grab it.

"Tep-a-ree Jones and his faithful dog Dusty waiting for the eclipse of the moon," I half-sang. "Picture House, New Mexico. Tep the Bean Man, the Human Bean, Dusty the dog, the old retriever, Old Faithful, waiting for the eclipse with her sidekick Tepary Jones."

I listened to the silence coming out of the ruin, silence so deep it seemed loud, and I waited for something to break it. I wondered if I'd hear from the great horned owl nesting high in the cliff above the ruin. I wondered if the ancestors of that owl nested in the same spot back when people had lived here.

The silence was broken at last by the scurrying feet of packrats coming to life now that day was done. Not all the residents of Picture House had abandoned their homes.

I fell asleep. I don't sleep much, but when I do, I sleep ferociously and my dreams often take strange shapes. Sometimes I wonder if they are dreams of the future. I could have used a glimpse of the future now, a dream to warn me away from Picture House.

Next thing I remember, Dusty was stirring. I checked on the moon and found it full as before, barely higher in the sky. I hadn't missed the eclipse. Suddenly I became aware of what Dusty already knew—voices were coming from the ruin. I was surprised and more than a little alarmed. We never ran into people up at Picture House.

I put my fingers to my lips. Dusty understood; we were old tracking partners. Once we even beat a mountain lion at her own game of watching without being seen.

Angling for a good vantage point, I crept a little closer, crouching behind the bushy junipers outside the big cave's drip line. Two voices. They were coming from inside the ruin all right, which rose like steps from one to two to three stories, all the rooms still perfectly preserved with even a couple of ladders connecting roofs and balconies. Picture House was lit up bright silver by the moon but still I couldn't see anyone in there. Then I heard a man's voice say, "This is going to be a five-thousand-dollar night." The second man laughed and said, "Ten-thousand-dollar night. This place has never been dug before."

I caught myself, hoping I'd heard wrong, but I'd heard what I'd heard. Pothunters! It felt like the wind had been knocked out of me, and I went down on my knees. I couldn't believe this was really happening. Picture House had never been vandalized before; it's the "last, best jewel," as my mother likes to put it, of all the cliff dwellings in the Four Corners states. The ruin isn't marked on maps, and it's sure enough hard to get to. But my folks had always said it was bound to get "bombed" one day.

I could hear the pothunters' shovels. I could see the bright light of their lanterns cast a hundred feet up on the arching cliff wall above the ruin. But we couldn't see the looters from where we were.

Sound doesn't carry into the wide cave anything like it carries out, so we had an advantage there. I crept closer, Dusty understanding the need to use the cover. My heart was pounding like thunder.

The voices were muffled now. I couldn't tell why. I held my breath and inched closer until I saw the shadow of one of the men, magnified by his glass lantern to forty feet or more against the cliff where hundreds of petroglyphs were chipped into the smooth red sandstone. It was this wall of pictures that had given the lost city its name. I'd stood right where that pothunter was standing more times than I can remember, trying to decipher the jumble of symbols on that wall: the crooked lines that could have been snakes or lightning or rivers, the upside-down human figures, the bear tracks, the bird-headed people, the bighorn sheep, the handprints, the gallery of spirits with all manner of strange headgear, the humpbacked flute player bringing up the corn with the power of his magic song.

The Hopi Indians over in Arizona still remember their name for the flute player, the far-walking magic person who brought the seeds from village to village, whose journeys are remembered on rock walls from Peru to Colorado. Kokopelli is his name. He must have been something, my father likes to say, to be the only person remembered by name from those ancient times. He must have been able to make corn sprout and grow before your very eyes.

I listened carefully. For a while all I heard was digging, the brutal ring of metal against stone. Sometimes pothunters even wrecked the pictures. If they wrecked Kokopelli, I—I didn't know what I would do. I didn't know if I should be running for help now or staying to watch a little longer, to see if I could get a good enough look at the men to identify them later.

The Picture House wall had two big Kokopelli petroglyphs, maybe eight feet apart, and they were facing each other. I always wondered why the people who made the petroglyphs usually gave Kokopelli antennas if he was supposed to be a human being. Between the Kokopellis were two spirals side by side, so close together they were almost touching. Surrounding the spirals there were corn plants, lots of corn plants. The two humpbacked flute players were bringing up the corn with their magic flutes.

Now I could see the man who was casting the shadow on the cliff. He was stocky, I could see that, but I couldn't make out his features under his hardhat. The bandanna over his nose and mouth partly concealed a dark beard.

There was a gun at his hip.

Chapter Two

The bearded man was pulling sticks and other packrat rubbish out of the narrow space between the cliff and the back wall of the room at the edge of the ruin. I realized that the bandanna was probably on account of hantavirus. Everyone anywhere close to the spot where New Mexico, Colorado, Utah, and Arizona came together at the Four Corners holds their breath around rodent droppings—the droppings of deer mice especially. My dad and I are pretty worried about my mother, but she's wearing a mask now when she's working in her lab. Hantavirus has killed eleven people within a hundred miles of here in the last six months, and before that nobody had even heard of it. For a couple of weeks after you catch it, they say, you don't even know you've got it. Once it breaks out, all it takes is forty-eight hours. Your lungs fill up with fluid, you can't breathe, and then you die.

These pothunters were so greedy even hantavirus couldn't scare them off. Sitting out in the open was a graceful pot they'd already dug up, probably a seed jar. It didn't look big enough to be a water jar. With its elaborate black-on-white designs, it would bring a lot of money on the black market.

Dusty whined ever so slightly when she saw the pot, and I gave her a look. The sight of a freshly dug pot was too much for her, I guess. Even so, I was surprised. She could've given us away if the pothunter hadn't been making so much noise dragging out the packrat rubbish.

I suppose all those memories of her glory days must've come rushing back and overwhelmed her with nostalgia.

Dusty wasn't ever trained to sniff out underground water jars, kiva jars, seed jars, and mugs and so on. She developed that knack herself back when my parents were working as archeologists. Try to get her to fetch sticks like an ordinary retriever—she had no interest.

The moonlight on Picture House seemed dimmer than before. With a glance over my shoulder, I found the moon already a quarter darkened. I'd missed the beginning of the eclipse!

Dusty whined again. This time the pothunter with the bandanna over his nose and mouth paused and listened, and his hand went to the revolver on his hip. There was only the sound of his partner digging inside the room

9

where the light of a second lantern was pouring out the keyhole-shaped doorway.

The man on the outside pulled his bandanna below his mouth. "Did you say something, Rodney?" he called, and was answered by a grunt from within.

I could picture the inside of that room, I'd been in there so many times. The smooth plaster on the back wall remained perfectly intact. It was decorated with a row of white triangles at eye level, like snowclad mountain peaks upside down. At one end of the row was a crescent moon; at the other, the moon was full.

I could guess why the pothunters were trying to get at the dead space between the cliff and the back wall of that room. The ancient people almost never built a back wall if the room backed up to the cliff—the cliff wall would do fine. They would only have built a back wall a little ways out from the cliff if they wanted to use the space in between for a purpose, like burying someone in there.

And with a burial the Ancient Ones almost always left pots.

The man inside the room must be opening up holes in that back wall, which rose about twenty feet before it met the curving cliff. He'd probably been robbing graves for years and knew exactly what he was looking for. I was hoping he was finding nothing for his trouble but packrat nests. I wondered if he knew that to paleontologists like my mother—scientists who study plants and animals that lived in the past—packrat nests are natural time capsules and scientific treasures.

Probably he hadn't heard that.

For five years now, my mother had been studying samples from a midden, a huge hanging rat-dung heap in a niche at the other end of the big cave. She thinks that the packrat middens might explain some of the mysteries of Picture House.

There aren't many paleontologists who do what my mother does. Lately they've come up with a name for her specialty: "paleonidology," the study of old nests.

I was trying to think if there was anything I could do to scare off the pothunters when I heard a big rumble, then glass breaking as the light inside the room was suddenly extinguished. Dust billowed out of the keyhole doorway and kept coming. The man had brought the wall down on himself!

All of a sudden the man on the outside was hollering and dancing straight up and down as three or four packrats ran out of the doorway and between his legs. They were bushy-tailed woodrats, big ones. Dusty had her head cocked, studying those rats running for cover, and I laughed under my breath at the sight of that dancing dirtbag.

The dust was clearing some. The man from inside emerged limping, all covered with dust, and tore off his bandanna. He had a drooping mustache. Both of them were in their late twenties. The man who was hurt was

11

coughing and swearing, limping around and trying his knee. "I got bit by a rat!" he was yelling. "Probably gonna get rabies! Probably gonna get hantavirus!"

"Rodney, you're lucky, considering. . . . I keep telling you to wear a hardhat."

The tall one slapped his crushed cowboy hat against his leg, making bursts of dust. "Tell me about it, Duke, you tell me all about it. . . . well, something fell out from behind the wall, right onto me. It felt disgusting. Go check it out."

The bearded man took the lantern inside and emerged a few minutes later with a small basket. He was almost giddy. "What fell in your face was a burial, Rodney. Awful well preserved, I'll tell you, but he kind of busted up when he fell. An albino, from the looks of him— pink skin. Looks weird enough, I'll tell you. There was a big pot that got broke, and this basket was inside it."

They started pulling objects out of the basket and setting them out on the bedrock at the foot of the picture wall. "Look at all this stuff!" Mustache shouted. "Crystals, arrowheads, shell beads, a stone pipe, some roots or something, porcupine teeth, a bone flute . . . and look at all these little pouches!"

"Medicine man's bundle!" his partner declared. "No doubt about it; our albino was a medicine man. We'll open the pouches later. Even our dad never found a medicine man's bundle!"

12

"Ten-thousand-dollar night, I told you, Duke! Maybe more!"

Just then the great horned owl up in the cliff hooted with that deep voice of hers, *hoo, hoo-hoo-hoo, hoo-oo, hoo-oo.*

"Spooky," one of them said.

Just after he spoke, their surviving lantern dimmed and then went out. "*Really* spooky," the other agreed.

The eclipse had devoured three quarters of the moon, and there was little light reaching the ruin. After the brothers had fumbled around for about five minutes, the same one who'd been hurt before started screaming that he'd just been stung by something. "Probably a scorpion!" he bellowed.

The man was screaming and cussing like he was going to die of the pain—I guess it really was a scorpion that got him. Our scorpions hurt like fire for a while but that's about it. I've been stung twice myself.

"This place is enough to make you believe in evil spirits," the hurt one wailed with a hollow laugh.

"But it's a gold mine," his brother replied.

I was thinking they could stand to see another omen—it might scare them off. All I had on me was my pocket knife and a little lighter; I always carry both of those. I got an idea and backed out of there with Dusty. Ten minutes' walk brought us to the foot of the steep slope that would lead to the top of the cliff above the big cave that housed Picture House.

It hadn't rained for about six weeks, so all the spring weeds had gone to seed and dried out fast. I found a tumbleweed as big around as a beach ball and dry as the top of a hot stove, and then started climbing for the top. The eclipse had darkened all but a sliver of the moon now and we had less and less light by the moment. But we knew the way so well, we climbed nearly as fast as we would have in daylight.

I knew the exact spot to stand at the edge of the cliff in order to make a drop that would land right in front of them. Holding the tumbleweed by its root, I lit it, then tossed the burning bush up and away from the edge. In the darkness of the eclipse it fell like a blazing meteor and I marveled at its beauty as it vanished below.

"Bet that caught their attention," I whispered to Dusty.

I was hoping I might see what direction the pothunters would take, if indeed they left. It was Dusty who noticed their flashlight beam far below. Indeed we had run them off. They were heading not toward the road that runs through the Seed Farm, but toward Enchanted Mesa where the tall pines grow. The mesa was crisscrossed with logging roads, and that's where they must have left their vehicle.

Returning to the ruin, I stopped only long enough to find that they'd taken the pot and the basket, as I would've guessed. But I did find one item from the basket that they'd overlooked and left behind: a small,

14

polished flute with three small holes toward one end and one toward the other. It looked to have been fashioned from a naturally hollow bone. Probably it was made from an eagle's wingbone. I should never have stood there admiring it. I should've returned it right away to the albino medicine man, but for one thing I was afraid of going in there and looking at him.

The more I held it, the more I wanted it for myself, at least for a while. The flute had already been taken from the medicine bundle, I told myself. If I returned it to the medicine man, the pothunters could come back and take it. If I kept it, I could protect it.

I could have hidden it somewhere, anywhere, but I didn't.

Feeling like something of a thief myself, I turned it over and over in my hands, imagining how ancient and powerful it must be.

Something told me I shouldn't put it to my lips. But I did anyway—I just couldn't resist. I blew on the single hole close to one end, and the flute surprised me with a sweet sound, pure and clean. The ages certainly hadn't dimmed its quality. I continued to blow as my fingers stopped the holes on the other end, one after another. Suddenly I recalled what I'd come here for and glanced up to see only an aura of light ringing a black disk—a total eclipse of the moon.

I flinched as I realized I was being watched. Not six feet away, two eyes reflected the dim starlight. I realized

I was looking at a big packrat with a squirrel-like tail— a bushy-tailed woodrat. Now I could even see its large eyes and whiskers and its prominent bushy tail as it stood on two legs. The rat seemed to be entranced by the notes from the ancient instrument.

I took the flute from my lips, worried a little at having drawn the rat so close. Packrats never come that close to people.

Again I considered stashing the flute in some safe place. But what if the pothunters came back and found where I'd hidden it? What if they were watching even now, and saw me hide it?

The flute was gleaming in the starlight, much too beautiful not to have for myself, if only for a while. I tucked it in my pocket and started home. Maybe I would tell my parents about it.

But maybe I wouldn't.

Chapter Three

By the time we got home the moon was riding high and the eclipse had passed. We stopped on the rim of the shallow canyon to admire the Seed Farm below. Living here we walked every day in the footsteps of the Ancient Ones. We were farming the same fields they had farmed.

The patchwork of our drylands crops on the canyon floor was all lit up silver and the tin roofing atop the old two-story cabin shone even brighter. It must have been two in the morning. My parents wouldn't mind me slipping in late; they'd encouraged me to make my hike and had planned on staying up for the eclipse themselves.

Since before I can remember my parents have been encouraging me to get out and explore. "A house is only a shelter," my father always likes to say. "Stay outdoors as much as you can." My mother's not the kind who worries—she's not afraid for me when I'm out hiking with Dusty. Riding in a car, that's what she thinks is dangerous, and I guess she's right. "I want you to love the Wild," she told me once. "You'll be fine if you stay cautious and use your good judgment. There's very little to fear out there but yourself."

Of course, that was before we had pothunters.

I left Dusty outside and slipped in the back door, climbed the ladder up to my room, shut the door behind me, and sat on my bed turning the bone flute in my hands. In the moonlight pouring through my windows the flute shone almost like it was lit from inside. I was deep in thought, wondering what hands had touched it and how old it might be, when the back of my head took a direct hit from our ringtail.

Ringo had sprung from one of the roof beams, made his strike, and was back in the rafters whisking his tail. Only half grown, sleek and tan, Ringo's body isn't much bigger than a squirrel's. But no squirrel can claim a tail to compare to this one, with its alternating black and white rings and its overall size. Ringo's tail is noticeably bigger than his head and body combined.

Ringo's large eyes are circled with white fur, which makes them seem even bigger. He's got a button nose, long whiskers, and a slender, cat-like body with delicate cat-like feet. Prospectors kept ringtails in their cabins to control rats and mice, and they called them ringtail cats, but Ringo's no cat. He's related to raccoons.

Now he sprang like a blur from rafter to rafter, down onto my bed, up to my shoulder, and onto the narrow window frame where he posed acrobatically, whisking his tail, studying me with those enormous, intelligent eyes. Ringo jumps me every week or so. I never know when to expect him—he covers a lot of territory outdoors as well as in. Sometimes he'll fly right into my chest, sometimes I get it in the back. Once he came shooting from under the bed and right up my pant leg.

Ringtails are night hunters. In addition to Ringo's night vision, he's got huge ears atop his little face, and I'd guess he can hear a mouse at fifty feet. Where he dens up in the daytime, I've never figured out.

When I found him orphaned in the cliffs near Picture House, I brought him home and fed him first from an eyedropper, then from a bottle. He gets into the house through my room on the second story, through a little hole next to a roof beam where I pulled the mud chinking out.

Our house is at least a hundred years old, made of squared logs chinked with abode mud. It's the old homestead cabin of the Montoyas, the family that lives a mile down the road. Before we had Ringo the house was overrun with mice. My mother's allergic to cats, so we relied on traps for battling the mouse hordes—sometimes those mousetraps would be going off like popcorn.

But then I found Ringo. Mom loves Ringo but she hardly ever sees him, since my parents sleep with their doors shut. She says she hears him sometimes. My mother doesn't sleep as soundly as my father, who wears himself out every day in the gardens.

Ringo's value around here skyrocketed about a month ago, when the news came out about what was causing the mysterious illness that had suddenly started killing people in the spring. It was a virus, and who would've thought that common, ordinary deer mice would turn out to be the carriers? They're the ones with the white bellies and white feet that I used to take out of our mousetraps all the time. Who would've thought you could catch a deadly virus by breathing the fumes from mouse droppings or even evaporated urine?

Aside from being a valuable mouser, Ringo does have his bad points. Like chewing holes in my socks—he does that a lot. Eating my pinyon nuts. He bats my fossils around, and he'd chew on them too if they weren't solid rock.

I turned my attention from Ringo to the ancient flute in my hands. It was only about four and a half inches long, so smooth, so ancient. . . . I was about to put the flute to my mouth when Ringo swooped down and knocked it free. The ringtail grabbed for it, but I'd already snatched it up. He sprang to my desktop a few feet away and started waving his tail like a battle flag.

I remember putting the flute to my lips and blowing

on it a minute or two. The notes I was producing sounded as pure as falling water. I remember starting to feel dizzy . . . the room started spinning and reeling, and I was bucking like I was being ripped open and turned inside out. Next thing I knew, I had the sensation of having long black whiskers radiating out from my face. These whiskers almost hurt, they were so sensitive. My nose was twitching. I was aware of an alien scent, musky, overpowering, and close.

By now I was in a panic at whatever was happening, and Ringo was looking at me differently, strangely, starting to make those high-pitched ringtail hunting noises that sound like crackling static.

I didn't feel anything like myself, and when I looked at my hands, I could see why. I was looking at the five-clawed fingers of . . . a rat. I felt the bottom of my spine moving, and out of the corner of my eye I could see a tail, a long, bushy tail.

I jumped from the bed to the floor, but Ringo jumped just as quick. There was only a foot between us, and there was murder in his eye. "It's me!" I yelled at him. "It's Tep!"

Chapter Four

I woke in a sweat, on the floor, swimming with confusion. The rising sun was pouring through the end of the loft. I struggled to my knees and tried to get my bearings. My books had been knocked out of the bookcase, my fossils scattered all around the floor.

I've had a lot of wild dreams, I was saying to myself as I picked up my sharks' teeth, the scallops and clams, the imprints of worm runs and extinct plants. *But this was the wildest ever.*

What an awful dream.

I like to keep my room in order—everything where it should be. Living with my parents has made me appreciate my own space. Downstairs it's a chaos factory. Picking all these things up and putting them away would help me to sort out what had happened here.

It seemed obvious that Ringo had done all this, that I'd somehow slept through it, but it seemed so vivid, the memory of the battle I'd fought with him in the night. The strangest part was, I'd been a packrat, a bushy-tailed woodrat. It had been a furious battle and pretty much one-sided. Mostly he'd had me on the run. If I hadn't been bigger than he was, he might have done me in.

Dreams can be so elaborate, and so strange.

Suddenly I recalled packrats running through the legs of the pothunter who wore a gun, and a packrat entranced by the sound of a flute I had put to my lips. Last night I'd thought those things had really happened, but now I wasn't so sure. When had this dream actually begun?

It had all seemed so real, and yet at the same time so dreamlike. . . . Now it all came flooding back: the voices of those men, the wall crashing, the lantern glass breaking, the grave of an ancient medicine man, the flute. . . . Duke, that was one of the pothunters' names. They were brothers. I could almost remember the other name.

I remembered that I was going to tell my parents about the pothunters when the morning came so they could call the ranger in Encantado. Now I didn't know what to do. If I'd really found a flute, where was it?

I looked under my bed, behind my dresser, all over. No flute.

I looked at myself carefully in the mirror. I bared my teeth. The looked normal enough, thank goodness. It was just so vivid, having those huge whiskers. I could distinctly remember giving Ringo a good bite right behind his head.

I spit again and again into the sink. I rinsed my mouth out. I felt contaminated. Dreams can be so real. This one was way too real.

What was the other guy's name?

I restored the cushion to the rocking chair in the corner of the room and sat down to think. I remembered jumping from the floor onto the chair during the battle with Ringo, and how unexpected it felt when the chair started rocking underneath me.

I needed to backtrack.

The blazing tumbleweed popped into my mind. Dusty had been at my side and watched it fall.

Go back before that, I told myself. Go back to before the pothunters. What had I been doing? I'd been waiting for the eclipse. We'd taken a swim, and we were waiting for the eclipse.

And I'd fallen asleep. Surely, none of it had happened. Not the pothunters, not the medicine man, not blowing on the flute, and not turning into a packrat. None of it had happened. It was one huge tangled dream.

Why would I have dreamed that I turned into a packrat?

Who knows? as my mother often likes to say. Maybe it's connected somehow to worrying about her spending so much time picking apart those black and gold globs of rat dung. Knowing that it's deer mice that are supposed to carry hantavirus doesn't seem all that reassuring. But as she points out, nobody's saying that it's packrats, ground squirrels, chipmunks, or any other kind of rodents.

Stop! I told myself.

My head was still swimming. What I wanted most was to go downstairs and get back to normal. I changed T-shirts and practically flew down my ladder. Dusty was waiting for me down there, lifting the broad crown of her head for me to pat. It was refreshing to see the living room a complete mess as usual, piled high with scientific journals and seed catalogs and books, and to wade my way through to the kitchen.

"Hi, Tep," my mom said brightly. "Want some juice?" It was so reassuring to find her just as happy to see me as ever. She always makes me feel not just like her kid, but like a special guest somehow.

I don't know what made me do it—I gave her a kiss on the cheek. I surprised myself and her, too, but she liked it. We were the same height now, and I hadn't done that in a long while.

"You certainly are bright-eyed and bushy-tailed this morning," she said.

I almost jumped out of my skin, but then I realized

25

she said that all the time. It was just an expression. Could she tell I'd had a rough night? I thought about telling her everything, but it was simply too weird. Some things you just can't tell your mother.

"Ringo must have paid you quite a visit."

"Yeah," I said cautiously. "He's crazy."

"There was one really big thump."

"Oh, that," I said. "I fell out of bed somehow."

My dad came sailing through from his morning run—he always runs up the valley to greet the rising sun. He had only his red jogging shorts and his running shoes on. He's a beautiful runner, graceful as a deer and tireless as a Tarahumara Indian—they're the famous long-distance runners down in Mexico that he admires.

In contrast to my mother, who keeps her hair short and neat, my father tends his about like a tangle of bean vines. I guess I'm more or less a hybrid: my hair's the color of my mother's—dark, like our eyes—but it behaves like his; that is, not at all.

"How was the eclipse?" my dad asked, curious and intense. When my father asks something, he really wants to know.

"Great . . ." I said. Usually I have a lot more to say than that.

"Did you see the whole thing?"

"Oh, yeah, it was a total eclipse," I assured him. "Didn't you?"

"I forgot to pull out the knob on the back of the clock after I set the alarm. We slept right through it!"

"Did you figure out any of the secrets of Picture House?" my mother asked playfully. Like me, she was sure that there were a number of mysteries to be answered there. Once she told me that some of the ancient pueblo people might have known as much about astronomy and time as Isaac Newton or even modern scientists like Albert Einstein and Stephen Hawking. I couldn't tell if she was serious or if this was what my dad calls her "mystical side" talking.

"I heard the owl up there," I answered evasively. The memory of last night's great horned owl had popped into my mind, but was it a made-up memory?

"Male or female?" my father asked.

"Female," I said. I'd learned from him to tell from their voices. "Her voice had that deep pitch."

"Bet she's got owlets to feed," my father said on his way to the bathroom.

I sat down to eat, all preoccupied. My mother brewed coffee and let me be. I was thinking about how to clear up my confusion. Before I told my parents any tales about pothunters up at Picture House, I had to go back up there and see for myself, though I dreaded looking inside that room. When it cooled off after supper, I'd go back.

My father talked over his coffee about how dry it had been, but how typical that was for June, the driest month

27

of the year. All our crops were dry-farmed, which means we never irrigated them. The idea was to plant rare vegetable seeds that can thrive in places where there's hardly any rain, and to produce a whole lot more drought-resistant seeds for people who subscribe to our catalog. My dad was all excited about a package of seeds he'd received the day before from Mister K.

We didn't have any idea who'd been sending us the seeds all this time because Mister K. never gave a name or a return address. My father guessed that he was a famous botanist who cherished his privacy—maybe a retired university professor. Whoever he was, he had a lot in common with the humpbacked flute player of ancient times, the legendary long-distance traveler who brought seeds from place to place. So my father had dubbed him "Mister K." in Kokopelli's honor.

For years now our Mister K. has been collecting rare seeds from the few dryland farmers who are still raising the old food crops, and he's been sending the seeds to us. We've gotten seeds from him mailed from as far away as Guatemala and as close as the Indian pueblos near Santa Fe. But we've never met him and don't have any idea how he ever heard of the Seed Farm. All we ever get is the seeds with something scribbled down about where they came from. We don't even know for sure if Mister K.'s ever seen our catalog, though we guess he has. We wonder if he's heard how his seeds are starting to get around now, even to foreign countries where they're desperate for crops that don't need a lot of water.

Mr. K. isn't our only source for seeds, but he goes back the farthest—six years, all the way back to our second summer. And his seeds have always been the most interesting to my father.

As my father was talking, he was letting some of the new seeds—golden tepary beans—run through his fingers and into a teacup. He loves to handle seeds, and so do I. There's something about the feel of them, especially beans. They're so smooth and shiny. "Mr. K. sent three new kinds of teparies," my father was saying, "plus a cushaw squash I don't think we've seen before, some kind of gourd seeds, and a sixty-day corn—all late-season varieties to plant before the rains."

It was my father who named me Tepary, after the beans. They aren't as big as a lot of beans, either as seeds or as plants, but they're the hardiest in the world. Teparies can sprout, grow, and bear on a couple of rains. In fact, we got a letter from one of our subscribers in Arizona who said one rain was all they'd had the summer before, but that's all our teparies had needed. Teparies have roots twice as long as any other bean and small leaves that turn all day to track the sun. I guess when I was born, my father thought I'd have to be awfully hardy to survive, like a tepary. Barely over two pounds, that was all I weighed.

My father poured the golden teparies back into a

small paper bag, which he returned to a basket with other bags full of seeds. "I'm going to start planting some of the seed that Mr. K. just sent, along with the others that need to go in before the rains come, if and when they come."

"They'll come," my mother assured him.

"For a scientist," my dad said to me, "your mother's got an awfully long optimistic streak. This is dry country. One of these summers the rain could skip us."

"Keep the faith," my mother replied.

My father reached out and hugged her close. "Faith is the Seed Farm's currency," he proclaimed. "It's certainly not cash!"

Absentmindedly, I was looking over the new seeds in the paper bags. Tepary beans, squash, corn . . . I could see from the shapes, sizes, colors, and markings that they were all slightly different from the varieties we already had. "Where's the gourds you mentioned?" I asked. "Didn't you say Mr. K. sent gourds?"

"It's too late to plant gourds."

I knew my dad was right. We'd planted gourds back in the first week of May. We raise them for people to make rattles and dippers from, and just for decoration.

"So why'd Mr. K. send them in June?" my mother wondered. "Isn't that when he sends seeds that can be planted late?"

"He always has before. . . ." my father agreed. He stroked his smooth chin and said, "I wonder if you're on to something." He went over to the clutter on the big table to retrieve the gourd seeds. "Maybe there's a message?"

Sure enough, he pulled a slip of paper out of the bag and held it up dramatically. "IT'S LATE, BUT PLANT THESE ANYWAY," he read, and then he declared, "Of course I'll do it. If Mr. K. said to plant them in concrete, I'd do it. I wonder . . . I wonder what they'll do."

My mother smiled to see him so intrigued. There were many sorts of things that made my father happy, and very high on the list was discovering a new variety of a plant that was somehow different from all its relatives. The length of its growing seasons was an important difference, like resistance to disease or how little water it could get by on.

"What a team we are," my father marveled as he caught my eye. "Without you and me putting in our two cents' worth, and your mother contributing a dime, we wouldn't have got these gourds in the ground today." With that he headed out the door.

My dad's first job would be to get the college students lined out for the morning. He always met them at Big Pink, the old adobe-mud house where they lived down at the far end of our fields. They were getting up early these days. When they first got here they'd slept in, but as June started warming up they caught on to how it wasn't so much fun to work in the heat of the day. They were all wild about working on the Seed Farm, for love and for college credit, but they weren't stupid. Now they even beat my father out to the fields sometimes.

I spent the day working on my raven defenses out in the corn patches, erecting poles all over and connecting them with a network of parachute cord to hang things from, whatever I could think of that might slow the ravens down this year.

No matter how hard I tried to keep my mind on what I was doing, I couldn't push my nightmare away. I kept wondering if there really was a corpse of an ancient albino medicine man lying in a heap of rubble up in that room at Picture House.

I had a pile of bones I'd been collecting behind the house; they rattle in the wind nicely and sometimes spook ravens. Late in the afternoon I was collecting a bunch to hang up on my lines when I discovered the eagle-bone flute in the pile. I stood there struck dumb to have it in my hands again. Obviously it was the same one. Ringo must have taken it from my room and left it here, I concluded. All of a sudden I was shaking. What if none of it was a dream?

I tucked the flute away in my pocket. I had a lot to think about. At supper I kept glancing at the note my father had stuck on the refrigerator just a few days before. It said, EAT THE BIG FROG FIRST.

I'm not sure what it meant to him, but the big frog at the top of my agenda was a return visit to Picture House.

Rodney, that was the other guy's name.

Chapter Five

Dusty and I approached the big cave cautiously, listening for voices. Then, from three different places, I watched. Picture House, with it forty-three rooms and its two towers, looked the same as ever. I began to breathe a whole lot easier.

But as I approached the red cliff with all the picture writings, boot tracks on the chalky ground brought my breath up short. There were tracks all over the place, and a lot of them weren't mine.

I listened, and Dusty did too. All I heard was the profound silence of Picture House.

Looking around, I wondered if I was being watched. I didn't think so.

I was stalling. Finally, I approached the keyhole doorway into the room nearest the petroglyphs. The edge of a mound of rubble was showing. I dreaded what I had to do, but if I was going to report a crime I had to know what I was talking about.

I paused outside the doorway, and tried to slow my heart down. If anything it beat faster: I bent and ducked inside.

What caught my eye first was the smashed lantern next to the mound of rubble. But in the next instant I saw the empty eye sockets of the medicine man, his long teeth in the gleaming jawbones, his blotchy pink skin drawn tight like rawhide across his forehead, his white-blond hair. He'd been buried with his knees drawn up against his chest, and so he remained, with shreds of a rabbit-fur blanket remaining here and there. His head was now separated from his body.

I held my hand to my nose and mouth, though the scent of decay was so slight I may have imagined it. At least the packrat midden jammed in the space behind the wall hadn't fallen out on him. It was still glued to the cliff.

The smashed pot that had housed the basket had fallen next to the medicine man. Its lid remained unbroken. Bits of the upside-down mountains that had been painted on the plastered surface of the wall lay here and there amidst the destruction. I stooped to pick up a piece of what had been the full moon, and then put it back where I had found it.

I had no business being here, looking on him, violating his secrecy. I should never have touched his flute. Last night I'd been a grave robber too.

I took the bone flute from my back pocket and placed it in the grip of his skeletal fingers. "I didn't mean any harm," I whispered. "Please let me be."

Dusty had remained in the doorway. I turned from the ancient corpse and we both went outside. The sun was setting and a dagger of light on the cliff wall caught my eye. It was cast by the fracture in a tall piece of rockfall out in front of the ruin. The dagger was moving down among the petroglyphs, and I watched its passage. I'd never noticed it before. The dagger of light passed halfway between the Kokopellis, exactly between the spirals, each a foot across. The spirals brought to mind the enormous eyes of an owl. I'd never noticed that before either.

The sun was squeezing down below the horizon. I had the dreadful premonition that what had happened the night before when I'd put that flute to my mouth might happen again. I tried to slow my heart. I'd returned the flute and everything was going to be okay.

I dashed around the ruin, trying to find if the pothunters had done any other damage. None of the other rooms had been dug, but at the upper end of the ruin, close to the cliff at the back of the cave, I found a pit that had obviously been dug recently. I realized that this was where the seed jar had come from, the one I'd seen them with.

Close to the pit lay a knee-high rock slab where the women of Picture House had ground their corn. Over the centuries they had worn five parallel grooves into the slab with the strokes of their *manos,* the smooth grinding stones held in the palms of their hands.

Behind the slab I noticed a small pile of golden corn kernels on the ground. The pothunters had dumped them out of the seed jar they'd dug up. I picked them up and examined them—I'd never found corn at Picture House before. The kernels looked just about the same as the ones we dry every fall and sort into seed packets for selling. But these were ancient.

Ever since I can remember, I've been trying to sprout seeds I've found around ruins. I've tried corn, I've tried squash, I've tried beans. Not a single seed has ever sprouted, but I keep trying. It's not supposed to be possible, because those kinds of seeds don't stay good for very many years. Their coats aren't thick enough or their insides tough enough.

The only way they can survive, as my father always likes to point out, is if people keep raising them.

But still, I've always had this dream that if I keep trying, if I just keep believing, one day I'd get some ancient corn or squash or beans to sprout and grow.

The sun was down now, and the eastern horizon was glowing where the moon was about to appear. I'd just said to Dusty, "Let's pick up this corn before the mice discover it," and stuffed a handful into my pocket.

That's when it happened. Whatever magic I'd gotten mixed up in with that medicine man and his flute, it had a hold on me now whether I'd given the flute back or not. I could feel those whiskers twitching. I was shaking all over, terrified to have it happening again, and there was nothing I could do to stop it.

Dusty cocked her head one way, then another, watching all this happen. "It's me!" I was telling her, as I'd told Ringo, but all that came out were squeaks.

Dusty put her nose right next to my face and whiskers, and sniffed me carefully. I froze. Her face loomed gigantic in front of me. I was overwhelmed by her scent, the scent of an enemy.

I panicked, and dove into a cluster of sharp rocks.

I could hear her coming and going, looking for me. I thought my heart would explode, it was beating so fast. After a while I made my way into a niche in the cliffs, where I began to squeeze through a narrow passage. It led through a maze of sticks bristling with cactus spines into an opening lined with soft grasses. What was I going to do now?"

A moment later all I could think of was food. I could detect the smell of it nearby, and the pangs in my stomach were unbearable. I crept forward in the darkness through another passage, feeling my way with the whiskers as my eyes adjusted to the murky light. The passage led to an enormous mound of pinyon nuts. I picked one up in my hands and began to chew as fast as I could. I'd eaten only half of the nut when I heard, close and loud, a terrible drumming. I looked up to see a packrat beating out a warlike message with its hind foot. The rat bared its teeth, sharp as swords.

The next thing I knew there were three of them after me, maybe more. Squeaking and biting at my backside, they chased me out of there. I ran for my life.

Once in the open I ducked inside the closest room in the ruin, and then I fled from one to the next looking for shelter. Everywhere I went I ran into packrats carrying things around, dropping this and picking up that. As soon as they'd see me, they'd run me off. At last I found a dark corner to hide in, but as soon as I felt safe, all I could think about was my stomach, which was cramping. I had to find something to eat.

Then I remembered. Out by the pits the pothunters had dug, there was corn.

I came out into the silver moonlight, and I soon found the corn. I never stopped to think why none of the rats had discovered it yet; I was only grateful they hadn't.

The corn was good. I was intent on eating every bit of it. I never paused to figure out why none of the packrats were showing themselves in the moonlight.

Suddenly I saw Dusty, from nowhere, leaping toward me. I recoiled, certain I was going to die.

But it wasn't me she was after—she was leaping into the air above me. Then I saw the reaching talons below wings wide as the sky. Dusty knocked that owl from the air a moment before it would have snatched me, pierced me through, and flown me to its young. I hadn't heard that bird coming, not one hint. Silent death, that's what that great horned owl would have been.

With a mighty rush of wings, it flew away.

Dusty put her great face next to mine. This time I wasn't afraid. *She knew me.* How else could I explain it? Dusty *knew* it was me. I stuck close to her the rest of the night. We curled up together, and I slept.

As the sun was rising, the magic broke loose and gave me back myself in an exploding moment of transformation, just as it had the day before. Dusty watched it happen again. She wagged her tail, and I patted her on the head. I thanked her for saving my life.

Was this going to happen all over again with the setting and rising of the sun? I dreaded that it would.

This is your own fault, I told myself. You wanted to find ancient secrets, now you've got one.

I had to get myself free of the magic. That flute, I thought, that medicine man's flute is the key. The flute had turned me into the nearest living creature—the packrat who'd come close to hear those first notes I'd made. I wasn't sure about anything really, but I had a feeling I'd better go back to the corpse and get that flute. If the flute could do this, I had to hope it could undo it as well.

I ducked back through the low doorway of the pillaged room. The medicine man was still there, but the flute was gone from the bones of his fingers.

My first thought was that the pothunters had returned during the night. But I saw no new footprints. Then I realized that the packrats must have taken it. Trader rats, that's another of their names, because of the way they'll drop one object for another, seeming to make a trade. And here, by the albino's hand, was a matchbook a rat might have dropped when it picked up the flute. The matchbook was from the Hacienda Motel in Encantado. Had the pothunters dropped it nearby the other night? Were they staying right in Encantado, only seventeen miles from the Seed Farm?

I pocketed the matchbook. Maybe I could find the flute later. For now all I wanted was to head home. I'd show the matchbook to my parents and tell them about the pothunters, the sooner the better. Then I'd have to tell my story to the sheriff and the Bureau of Land Management ranger too. How was I going to explain waiting a day to report the crime?

What a mess I was in.

How was I going to explain to my parents why I had just stayed out all night?

I could say I'd found the matchbook the night before, when I was up at Picture House for the eclipse, and that I went back because I got to worrying that someone might be hanging around up there, up to no good. Then, when I returned, I saw everything that really I'd seen the night before. Only the pothunters would know they had committed their crime the night of the eclipse. It was going to be the best I could do. I'd never had much practice lying.

I could have dropped in my tracks, I was so tired. At last Dusty and I reached the rimrock above the Seed Farm. The sun had already sailed pretty well up in the sky. We could see my father and the college students planting down below.

What a mess.

Chapter Six

"**P**icture House has been bombed!" I told my mother, and she had me run for my dad. I told them everything I thought I could tell them, and it made them sick. They worried that the pothunters would return again and soon. My dad called the Bureau of Land Management ranger in Encantado, and tried to put me on the phone, but I guess the ranger didn't want to talk to a kid unless he had to. I was relieved. My dad told him everything just the way I had said it; he even remembered to mention the matchbook. After all of that my father asked what was going to happen with the corpse of the medicine man.

My dad was slow to speak after he placed the phone back on the hook. "Well, what did the ranger say?" I asked.

My dad glanced from me to my mother, who was just as anxious. "He's trying to get ahold of the sheriff right away. He didn't sound hopeful. They never have much luck catching pothunters, much less convicting them. But he's going to send someone from the BLM office to watch Picture House, in case they come back."

"What about the medicine man?"

"He said he'd call one or more of the pueblos near Santa Fe. The elders will come and rebury the medicine man in some secret place—the ranger thought they'd try to get it done right away."

"This is really bad," my mother said. "I just hope those pothunters get caught. Let's hope they're still at the motel."

But when the BLM ranger called back twenty minutes later, we found out they were gone without a trace.

My father couldn't go back to work. He stewed all morning, trying to get ahold of the sheriff himself. I was so worn out I thought I might fall down on the floor. My mother was encouraging me to take a nap, but I had to know what was going to happen.

Finally, during lunchtime the sheriff called back. My dad was upset when he got off the phone.

"The sheriff said they were obviously professionals, and they're no doubt long gone by now, probably in another state. They used false names at the motel, but with Tep providing their first names and their physical descriptions, plus the fact that they were brothers, the

43

computer just might spit out who they are—especially if they have a history of pothunting. Even so, the sheriff said it's really hard to get a conviction in these kinds of cases. Hates to waste his time, he kept saying.''

"But I saw the whole thing!" I objected. "I can say where they got the seed jar and the medicine bundle. They dug them up on public land, and that's a federal crime!''

"You're right," my dad said. "I agree with you. But the sheriff said that just your word wouldn't be enough. They'll need proof—they'll need the seed jar and the medicine bundle. I guess he's tired of all these cases just getting dismissed in court. But he did say that if they happen to catch those guys and recover the artifacts, this time they won't be able to claim they dug them up on private land. That's what usually happens. You'll be a witness that they dug them on public land, and then they'd be convicted.''

My mother and my father began to talk about the fine points of the pothunting laws, and a minute later I gave in to my weariness. My elbow slipped off the edge of the table and my soup spoon fell to the floor. I caught my head falling sideways and snapped back awake. Dusty was licking the spoon, and my parents were smiling.

"You're exhausted," my mon said. "Why don't you go to sleep now?''

"I think I will," I agreed. "Soon as I take a shower.''

I was going to scrub a long time, to see if I could somehow wash off this whole mess. I was already wondering if the packrat had given me hantavirus.

"Good job, Tep," my dad said. "I love how you scared them off with the flaming tumbleweed."

I nodded dumbly, unable to take any satisfaction in this whole episode.

I slept the afternoon away. In the early evening I woke up, relieved in the moment I awoke to find myself in my own body. But then, the sun hadn't gone down yet. I found my parents working at the big table, answering letters from fans of our seeds and addressing the labels on seed packets that were going out in the next day's mail. I mustn't have looked very good. "Are you feeling sick?" my mother worried. "Can I get you anything? Some soup? Tea with honey? We're going to have dinner after a little bit."

"I feel fine," I said, but really I wondered if I was starting to get hantavirus. On top of that, I was full of dread that I might turn into a packrat once again.

"I know how sad you are about Picture House," my mother added.

"It's not just that. . . ." I said.

Both my parents were looking concerned. "Can you tell us?" my mother probed gently.

I thought about it. I really thought about it. But I shook my head. "I'm just tired, I guess."

"Even nighthawks need some sleep," my father said helpfully. "You have a lot to catch up on."

After supper, I excused myself before dessert. I'd been watching the sun carefully, and it was dropping low. With a heavy heart, I climbed the ladder.

My last glance before I closed the door on the landing of the loft was of Dusty down at the bottom of the ladder, looking up at me solemnly with those huge brown eyes of hers. Old Faithful. Was she wondering if it would happen to me again tonight?

I shut the door behind me and got to work on what came first: plugging up Ringo's entry hole. I wedged a chunk of petrified wood in there, and it fit perfectly.

Now, what of my own things did I need to protect from the rat? I didn't have any food in my room, that's what he'd go for first.

That's when I remembered the seeds I'd brought from Picture House, the ancient corn I was going to plant before the summer rains came. The handful of kernels was still in my jeans, which I'd thrown in my dirty-clothes basket. I retrieved the seeds and sealed them in an old fruitcake tin where I kept my dad's very first tepary beans and other small treasures I'd collected over the years. I jammed the lid down extra tight.

Looking for some hope, my thoughts drifted up to Picture House. I hoped that the Indian elders had come this evening, that they'd already hid the medicine man away somewhere. If they said the right words, then maybe the magic would let me go.

It wasn't fair, I thought, that I was paying for the pothunters' crime. They were the ones who should have turned into packrats. I lay in bed shivering, terrified, as my room darkened and it happened again.

I can't say I wasn't responsible for the rampage that followed, because I saw it all happening. But it felt as if I was looking through a tiny window. It didn't seem my willpower could begin to resist the cravings and compulsions of the rat.

The first thing I went after was the corn inside the fruitcake tin. I was clawing and scratching at the lid trying to pop it loose. Finally I had to give that up, but then I started carrying things around in a frenzy, picking one thing up and dropping another. Every small object in the room was ending up in one corner, I didn't even know why. When I'd made a pile of everything from my room that was portable, I squeezed under the door and onto the landing.

Fortunately my parents had gone to bed. Dusty had been put outside for the night. If she'd been indoors, maybe she'd have saved me somehow from making such a fool of myself.

All the lights were out, but a packrat's large eyes are made for the dark, and I scurried down the ladder in search of anything I might bring back to my pile. Carried away in all the excitement and confusion, I must have made a hundred trips up and down that ladder. I'd find something that looked perfect, like a book of stamps, and then I'd drop it in favor of something else, like a spool of thread. On top of my parents' desk I discovered the seed packets that had been prepared for the mail, and I chewed into them voraciously, eating some seeds, spilling others, packing some upstairs.

And then, halfway up the ladder, I dropped a spoon. It crashed on the cabin's wood floor, and I ran the rest of the way up the ladder. The light came on with a blinding glare. I froze, trembling. It was my mother, and she was looking right at me, up on the landing.

She smiled a curious half-smile, and then she turned off the light and went back into their room.

Chapter Seven

When dawn came and I was myself again, I woke to find a mound in the corner of my room made of Popsicle sticks, pencils, pens, most of my fossils, my socks and underwear, my toothbrush, everything that had been in the trash can by my desk, my father's truck keys, stuffing from the couch downstairs, a squashed aluminum can, paper clips, rubber bands, torn seed packets, two dimes, three nickels, and a fork. In another corner of my room I found a pile of seeds. I was appalled. I picked up the fruitcake tin, which had been knocked to the floor. There were scratches all over it, but the lid had held.

Over and over, as I put my things back in place, I asked myself, *What am I going to do?* I threw the toothbrush in the trash. Fortunately I had another one up in my medicine cabinet.

I hated having to go downstairs. I didn't want to know what it looked like down there. But I knew I'd have to face it sooner or later.

At first glance, downstairs didn't look more of a mess than usual. But my dad was picking seeds off the floor and sorting out the ones strewn around on the table. "Looks like we had a visitor last night," he said, and he wasn't pleased.

"I even *saw* him," my mother chimed in from the kitchen. "A bushy-tailed woodrat!"

"Your mother thinks they're adorable," my father said. "Her partners in science! She didn't wake me up because she was afraid I might do him some damage. Where was Ringo?"

I looked around and my eyes quickly found the hole in the couch where the stuffing had been pulled out. "I didn't let him in last night," I said. "I really needed the sleep."

"The rat didn't get under your door, did he?" my mother asked.

"He sure did," I answered cautiously. "He left a big pile of stuff in the corner." I fished my dad's keys out of my pocket and handed them over. "Including these."

"We've gotta get that rat," my father said firmly. "We don't know for sure about what-all carries hantavirus. Look at these droppings on the table!"

My eyes went to the tabletop, and I cringed.

"Let's for sure give Ringo the run of the house to-night," my father said.

My mother looked doubtful. "I don't know if Ringo's big enough to take on that rat. It looked full-grown to me, maybe two feet long counting the tail."

"Traps," my dad said. "That's what we'll do."

"Live traps," my mother insisted. "We can move him down the road, but let's not kill him."

At breakfast I chewed my cereal very slowly. My father was going to be after me. He was worried that I could infect everybody with hantavirus, and he was right to worry. I had to move out. Since I had to let Ringo back indoors anyway, I didn't have any choice. "You know," I told them, "It's getting kind of hot upstairs—too hot to sleep."

"It's that time of year," my mother agreed. "Are you going to start sleeping under the stars again?"

That's what I usually did once summer heated up. If the rains came, I'd pitch my tent. I didn't have much time to think about it, but I was scared to death picturing myself sleeping in the open now, or even in a tent. I said, "I think I'll try the Silver Bullet."

The Silver Bullet was the ramshackle little travel-trailer halfway up the fields toward Big Pink, the old mud house where the college students lived.

The stairs down to my mother's lab in the basement are outside the house. The storm doors just above ground level were thrown open for ventilation. It was midafternoon and hot, and I knew it would be cool down there. But mostly I just wanted to talk. Once, when I'd asked my mother if she believed in magic, she'd said something like, "There's more on heaven and earth than is dreamt of in our philosophy." I'd asked, "What does that mean?" She replied, "There's a whole lot more that we *don't* know than what we *do* know."

My mother looked up when she saw me coming down the stairs. She was at her desk, picking at a baseball-sized packrat glob with tweezers and a dentist's pick. She was wearing her mask, but when she saw me she wheeled away from her work and took it off. "Hi, Tep," she greeted me, cheerful as ever. "Have you seen my 'partner in science,' as your dad calls him—or her?"

It's a him, I thought painfully. "He must be lying low," I replied. "Probably he heard dad talking about him."

"I have a bet with your father that our bushy-tailed woodrat is much too smart for that old live trap of his. All he ever caught with it was a skunk, and you remember how that turned out."

I laughed, remembering. I said, "You really do like those bushy-tailed woodrats?"

"Oh, absolutely. You should have seen the one last night. His whiskers were as long as your little finger. He's got a rich, reddish-brown coat on his back, a white underside, white hands, and the tail is precious. You know there are six species of packrats all together, and the other five have those naked tails.''

"Those'd be disgusting," I said.

"I agreed. The one in the house was bushy-tailed, that's for sure, just like the ones up at Picture House, where this specimen came from." With a nod, she indicated the yellowish lump on her worktable. "If it weren't for the hantavirus scare, and for Ringo of course, I'd love to capture our visitor and keep him for a pet."

"Oh yeah?"

"Sure. We'd have to keep him in a cage, though, and it'd be a shame to take away his freedom."

I was so disturbed by the idea, I could only nod in agreement as I was looking around at her lab. "You've got a good breeze going through here. What *about* hantavirus? Could it be in this stuff you take apart?"

"I really don't think so," my mother assured me. "This stuff is so old it'd be like catching a virus from an ancient Egyptian mummy."

I thought about the ancient corn from Picture House that I wanted to sprout. "But is it possible?"

"I suppose it's possible," she admitted. "But really, there are a lot of people at the Centers for Disease Control in Atlanta who are working on the hantavirus outbreak, and they're all pointing their fingers at the deer mouse."

She took a clipping from her bulletin board and handed it to me. "You'll enjoy this," she said. It was from one of her scientific journals. "Read the part I highlighted. It's quoted from the diary of a lost prospector in the gold rush of 1849."

I read it out loud:

Part way up we came to a high cliff and in its face were niches. . . . and in some of them we found balls of a glistening substance looking like pieces of candy. . . . it was evidently food of some sort, and we found it sweet but sickish, and those who were hungry, making a good meal of it, were a little troubled with nausea afterwards.

"That's sick," I said, with great appreciation.

"I knew you'd like that."

My mother hardly ever talked about what she was doing, nothing compared to how much we all talked about our seeds. She didn't want my father to find out about her conclusions until she could surprise him. I asked her, "What all's in this 'candy' that you study?"

"Well, all sorts of things: sticks, plant fragments, bones, animal dung, and their own pellets of course. They're great collectors, and they bring back to the nest all the trash they can find—collectibles, I'd guess you'd have to say, from their point of view. Of course, everything gets saturated with urine, which evaporates and crystallizes, making a big, hard lump over time. Did you know packrats have been living at Picture House for about forty thousand years?''

"No kidding? Forty thousand years is a long, long time.''

"They started the midden I'm studying about thirty-eight thousand years before the pueblo ancestors arrived at the cave and started building pit houses. That's what the radiocarbon reports I get back are telling me. Carbon-14 breaks down at a perfectly continuous rate, so it's a marvelous tool. The natural radioactivity in anything organic—the plant fragments, the fecal pellets—tells quite a story. Tep, what I've been doing is like making a movie, really. I've been taking samples from the midden, dating them, looking at the changing picture of what grew and what animals lived within two hundred feet of the nest—that's the range of a packrat.''

"That's the part I never really understood,'' I confessed. "I mean, where does that get you?''

"People lived at Picture House for a thousand years,'' my mother said solemnly, "and then they went away. Why? The packrats might provide the answer. I'm trying to find out what grew here before the people moved in, and how that picture changed during the time they were here—not just around the cave, but two miles and four miles and six miles away as well. I'm studying four different packrat middens altogether. I want to see if the people changed their own environment while they were here."

"And the packrat middens are going to tell why the people left?"

"Why they left might be a puzzle with a number of pieces, but packrat nests might give us an important one."

"Are you getting close?"

"*Real* close."

I gave her a little poke with my elbow. "You can tell me. I won't tell Dad."

"You know how scientists are—I have to be sure. I hope other paleontologists will study middens at other ruins around the Four Corners. It's so unusual, what happened in this region. Between about the years 1000 and 1250 thousands and thousands of sites were abandoned. Every single one. There's a lesson there for us today, I'm sure of it."

"You got a book on packrats I could borrow?"

She reached for her bookshelf and put her hand on one, just that fast. "Sure, here's my *Field Guide to Southwestern Mammals.* It has a section on ringtails, too."

I'd intended to climb up into the cottonwood tree a little ways down the creek, sit in my favorite spot, and read up on bushy-tailed woodrats, but a commotion up toward Big Pink caught my attention. Heading that way,

I could see Dusty was in the middle of it. The college students, standing around her in a circle, were sure excited about something. Carlos had seen me coming and was waving me over. "Tep, hurry up! You aren't going to believe this!"

What I saw was Mickey and April, on their hands and knees, working in the dirt with knives and forks and spoons, excavating a perfect black-on-white pitcher.

Chapter Eight

Those college students loved Dusty before, but now she was their absolute hero. "We were all sitting on the porch," Heidi reported breathlessly. "I noticed Dusty poking around and then digging. She kept looking at us like she wanted us to check out what she was doing, so I did."

Heidi had long red hair and a nose ring, but her distinguishing feature was her large eyes. When she was excited, like she was now, the whites showed all the way around and made them seem even bigger. "She was digging so delicately. I could see something circular, and then I realized I was looking at the top of an ancient pot!"

Now April and Mickey had the pitcher free, and April held it up. It was a beauty, all right, with a parrot's head atop a perfect handle. The body of the pitcher was decorated with connected spirals that looped gracefully from one to the next.

"*Dus*-ty . . . ," I said reproachfully. The old girl bowed her head and hung her tail and looked away from me toward her admirers.

"My father spent a couple years convincing her to quit digging pots," I explained.

They all broke into grins. Carlos was pulling on his beard and laughing.

"I'm not kidding," I said, and I told them all about Dusty's exploits in her younger days, on the big archeology project up in southwestern Colorado when I was little. My parents were part of a team that was trying to save what they could of a big site along the Dolores River before the dam was finished and the reservoir started to fill. There's a museum on the hill above the lake today; we've gone back twice to visit. Half the pots on display are Dusty's and there are a whole lot more in the basement.

"But how does she do it?" Buzz insisted.

"Ask my dad. He's got a theory—he thinks she can smell the pigment in the black dye they used for the designs."

Carlos still wore that grin, "Sure, Tep."

"Where *is* his dad?" Mickey asked. "Let's ask Art. I want to hear this firsthand, about Dusty, the pot-sniffing dog."

April pointed up the field. "I saw him just a little while ago, over in the Tarahumara garbanzo beans."

"Where's that?"

"Over by the Aztec corn."

I said, "Hey, don't you guys believe me?"

Heidi was watching me close with those big eyes. "Tep's pulling our leg. Remember when he told us about the magpie who could talk?"

I guess I had all those college kids from Ohio wondering. They don't know me that well—I'm not any good at making things up. I'd heard from the Montoyas down the road that you could teach a magpie to talk, and I thought I'd give it a try with a young one I'd been feeding. I had to keep at it, but Maggie learned to talk just fine. Magpies are related to crows and ravens, they're all big talkers. Maggie used to call my name a lot, and she even had a few expressions, like *What's to eat?* and *Pass the salsa!*

It turned out that Maggie had a fondness for bright and shiny objects, like thimbles and spoons and jewelry, especially my mother's earrings. You couldn't set anything down. Sometimes they'd turn up in out-of-the-way hiding places, sometimes they'd never turn up. After a while I tied Maggie by the foot with a long string I attached to a platform on top of a post.

Maggie didn't think much of being tied. She flew away with a bunch of her kind only a month ago, just a few days before the students rolled in for the summer.

The last time I saw her she was flying over the field trailing that string, and she was calling *"Tepary! Tepary! Tepary!"* I don't know if it's just because I was feeling guilty, but it sure sounded like she was scolding me the way she said it.

When my father returned from the garbanzos, he verified my story about Dusty's illustrious career as an archeologist. He wasn't too pleased about her having had a relapse, and gave her a good talking-to.

My dad had to decide what to do about the pitcher. The students all wanted to know what was going to happen to it. Since it was on our land it was legal to dig it up and legal to keep it, but my father wasn't keen on people digging up artifacts unless they were part of a full-blown scientific dig that was going to do it right. It was like tearing a page out of a book. Since the pitcher was already dug, and they promised to take good care of it, Dad finally agreed it could stay in Big Pink where the students could admire it all summer.

I spent the rest of the afternoon moving some things into the Silver Bullet, and then I grabbed the *Filed Guide to Southwestern Mammals* and climbed up into my favorite reading spot, up in the forks of the biggest cottonwood along the creek. Twenty feet off the ground, in the shade of that grandmother cottonwood, it's cool in the hottest part of the day. The slightest breeze gets all those leaves rustling, and it's the closest thing the Seed Farm's got to air conditioning.

Dusty was lying down below in the center of the big tree's shade patch, panting with her eyes closed. I turned to the field guide and quickly found the bushy-tailed woodrats. There was a great deal I wanted to know, and I plunged into it: "The soft, thick fur varies in color . . . the head has the same shape as other packrats, yet looks somewhat different owing to extremely large ears and long, silky whiskers up to four inches in length. The large, beady eyes are typical of packrats. Full-grown, these woodrats measure as much as twenty-four inches from the tip of the nose to the tip of the tail. Their entire appearance, from head to handsome tail, is entirely charming."

My mother could have written this, I thought, and read on: "The young, from two to six, are born in early summer. Compared to other small rodents, the reproductive rate is low, yet so is the death rate, due to the animal's secretiveness and high order of intelligence."

Intelligence, I thought. At least I'm turning into something smart.

"Their nest is a veritable fortress of sticks, rocks, bones, and often cactus, arranged to prevent entrance to unwanted visitors, which may include other woodrats. A maze of passages leads to the sleeping area, perhaps a foot in diameter, lined with soft and warm materials. Caches of food are stowed nearby. A third area serves as a rubbish heap and toilet. The woodrat's home has a strong, musky odor, but this is not an indication of uncleanliness. The creature is quite fastidious in its habits.''

I was happy to hear that. But the next part didn't sound good at all: "It's diet consists mainly of pine nuts, acorns, seeds, herbs, berries, fruits, and many other vegetable sources, sometimes even insects. Around a farm they can be real pests, destroying crops in their pursuit of food.''

Would that be next? I'll be destroying our crops?

Just then my mother appeared at the base of the tree. "I've got some good news and some bad news for you, Tep.''

At first I thought it was something about me. I didn't know whether to be scared or relieved. I looked down with my face blank and waited for what she would say.

"The good news is that they found out who the pothunters are. They turned out to be Rodney and Duke Bishop, from an infamous pothunting family in southwestern Colorado. The BLM there knows all about them. Apparently it's well known up there that neither they nor their father has ever done anything else for a living but dig pots.''

"Did the sheriff find them?''

"Driving their pickup through Encantado—they were still here.''

"Did they have the seed pot? The medicine bundle?''

My mom was shaking her head. "That's the bad news. They didn't have any artifacts with them.''

"Well, that doesn't mean anything—they must've stashed 'em somewhere. The sheriff or the BLM just has to find them."

"The sheriff says he doesn't have the manpower to be out searching the boondocks for pots. Meanwhile the Bishop brothers appear to have gone back to Colorado, but the BLM's going to keep somebody up at Picture House a little while longer just in case."

My mother left to pick some greens for dinner. She was going to deep-fry some squash blossoms, one of her specialties, to make me feel better.

I had a bad feeling about the night to come.

Chapter Nine

Dusk found me all moved into the Silver Bullet, door locked from the inside, windows closed. It was going to be a cooker in there, but I knew I had to keep those windows shut. The rat would chew or claw right through the screens.

Dusty was curled up right outside the door. I was lying on my back, on the bed, under a sheet drawn up to my chin. I was gripping the sheet with both hands, concentrating fiercely, trying by force of will not to let it happen again. "I am not a rat," I kept repeating to myself. "I am not a rat. My name is Tepary Jones, the Human Bean. I am not a rat. *I am not a rat.*"

As night fell the transformation struck, and my desperate voice turned to squeaks. I was looking at my whiskers again, and small hands with white fur and claws were clutching the sheet.

This time I was going to fight it, before the rat got the better of me. "My name is Tepary Jones," I hollered. *"My name is Tepary Jones!"*

No matter what it took, I told myself, I was going to stay in this bed. *You will sleep in this bed until the dawn comes. You are not going to scurry around this trailer all night, you are not going to scurry around this trailer all night. . . .*

It was unbearably hot and stuffy in that trailer. Lying on my back was torture. I threw off the sheet first thing. I tried curling into a ball on my side, but the rat and I were both nocturnal, and our minds were wide awake. I tried curling into a ball on my other side. All the while I was screaming with boredom. I was trapped. I've always hated being cooped up. I tried sleeping flat on my stomach, but I've never been able to do that. This is what it must have been like, I thought, when I was in the incubator, stuck in that tiny glass box. I could almost remember not being able to turn myself over. . . .

I had to get out!

Springing out of bed, I climbed up the curtain and perched on top of the curtain rod, looking around the trailer. I tried the windows I could reach, hoping one could be budged, but they were all shut tight and locked. I jumped to the kitchen sink, then to the floor, and I looked inside the cabinets. Something smelled like food. . . . green pellets inside a paper box. Sniffing them carefully, I realized something wasn't right about them, and then I remembered my father had put them in here for the deer mice. Around and around the trailer I went, trying to find anything that was interesting. There was nothing in there, nothing to eat, nothing to do. I had to find a way out. I couldn't help it. I just couldn't help it.

Back under the sink, I checked where the pipes ran through the floor, but the cracks were all stuffed with steel wool. I had stuffed it there myself! I tried gnashing my way through the steel wool, but all those bits of metal hurt like fire. I had to quit when a piece got caught in my throat and I started gagging. At last I coughed it up.

There had to be another way. Then I realized I was looking right at it—a slight dome of pressboard flooring that had raised up when we'd had a leak several years before. The floorboard might be rotten here!

The rat's teeth proved me right. It took some work, but finally I was free.

Dusty was waiting. She must've heard me chewing my way out. I approached her cautiously, then stood on two legs. Her eyes were locked onto mine. She sniffed me thoroughly, and she knew me.

I was ravenous, but I felt compelled to find shelter first. I headed up behind the trailer to the nearby rim-rock, a cliff twenty feet high that runs all along the top of our shallow valley. Investigating every cranny I could find, I found a niche that felt right, and I began to drag rocks and sticks in there.

A fortress began to take shape, complete with cactus spines in the narrow runways. I didn't have to think about the construction. The rat knew the blueprint by instinct. I watched him working through that tiny window in my mind.

Ringo was watching too, hoping and waiting for a chance to get at me. I could see his eyes shining in the dark as he paced back and forth. Dusty ran him off a couple of times, and I was able to work all night.

"How'd you sleep?" my mother asked over breakfast.

Could she tell I was exhausted?"

"Not very well . . . ," I replied. "It's too hot in the Silver Bullet." I hated saying these things that sounded true but weren't the truth at all. An old saying my parents had taught me kept coming to mind: "Oh, what a tangled web we weave, when first we practice to deceive."

"Why don't you sleep under the stars?" my father suggested. "I'd sleep outside if I could get a good night's sleep."

"I think I will," I agreed.

My mother glanced playfully at my dad. "Your father didn't catch the packrat last night."

"Oh, I'll catch him," my father assured her. "As far as I can tell, he wasn't back in the house last night."

I said, "I read in Mom's book that they're pretty smart."

"He better be. He'll be back. It's a matter of time."

After lunch I fetched my ground cloth and sleeping bag—not that I'd need them—and stashed them up in the rimrock, in a crack and under an overhang. Then I took a nap. I woke up late in the afternoon when I heard a car's brakes squeak down by the house.

It was Mrs. Montoya, our neighbor from down the road. Usually she called on the phone, so I knew this was important if she wanted to talk about it in person. I ran down and heard her telling my mom about something she'd heard on the radio.

"What is it?" I interrupted. Her face was all pale.

"Hantavirus! Right in Encantado! He was only thirty-four years old!"

"He already died?" my mother ventured.

"No, but he's on the way to the hospital in Albuquerque. They say it took forever for the helicopter to come. I wonder if he'll even make it to the hospital. Sometimes they die on the way, you know."

"And they seem to die when they get there too," my mother said.

"I know! It's awful!"

In the night, I divided my time between adding to my fortress and scavenging things to eat: juniper berries, pinyon nuts, last year's cactus fruit, almost any sort of

69

wildflower. Everything tasted good, I couldn't help it. I even found myself capturing beetles and spiders.

The next morning we turned on our radio. The thirty-four-year-old man from Encantado had died in the hospital in Albuquerque. His lungs had filled with fluid and the hospital hadn't been able to stop it.

My father, who was habitually cheerful, ate his breakfast in silence. All three of us were trapped in our thoughts. By lunch nothing had changed. The gloom held until my father came running in for his afternoon break with the news that the gourd seeds he'd planted only two days before had sprouted. "It's unbelievable!" he said. "Gourds should take at least a week to germinate!"

I returned to the fields with my father to have a look at the new gourds from Mister K. They'd already put out the first of their ragged, specialized leaves that follow the two rounded ones that did the groundbreaking. "I thought you said they just sprouted," I said to my father.

"They did, just this morning! I've never seen anything like it! No wonder Mr. K. said to go ahead and put them in the ground. Think how short their growing season must be! If you could isolate that gene, and apply it to other plants . . ." My father waded into gourd vines we'd planted from seed in early May and knelt down to inspect them, first the traditional varieties and then the wild gourds. He doesn't inspect the wild ones often, because the vines of wild gourds always leave a rank smell on your trousers. "I think they might need a little side dressing," he said.

A "side dressing" meant manure, and manure was my department. Anything having to do with manure, from cleaning out the chicken coop to applying side dressings, that's my job. Some years ago my dad tricked me into being the Manure Specialist, and I haven't been able to unload either the title or the job since.

"Sure thing," I said, even though I usually kept my distance from the gourds. I needed something to feel good about.

"Hey, wait a minute," he said, scrutinizing the vines. "Looks like we've got Luperini beetles again."

I took a look myself. Here they were, those crazy little striped beetles that actually feed on the juices of wild gourds. I heard my father say once, in one of those night classes he gives the college students, that the chemicals in wild gourds are the most bitter substances known to mankind. I can attest to that. When I was younger, I took just the slightest taste, and I'll never forget it as long as I live.

Besides Luperini beetles, the only other creatures I know of that love the gourd vines are the bees who pollinate them. I guess the flowers must smell like heaven to digger bees. The diggers appear at first light and the gourd flowers open especially early, just for them. The females spend the night underground, while the males overnight inside the flower, hugging the styles. The male looks like a drunk hanging onto a lamp post.

According to my mother, a packrat ventures only two hundred feet away from its nest. But that very night my worst fears came true. I far exceeded that invisible limit, roaming at will through our fields. I felt safe because Dusty was at my side. Now the rat knew about all the good things to eat down there and overpowered my will to resist.

Next morning, while my father was making his run up the valley, I went to inspect the damage I'd done in the night. I was stricken by what I saw. I'd started on the Yaqui basil and the desert chia, then proceeded into the forest of amaranth greens. I'd nipped some black-eyed peas and lima beans, but none of that was very noticeable. It was the squash that was obvious, several dozen little fruits that were partially chewed or gone. The ones I'd hit—I wouldn't be able to watch them grow! Some of those squashes would've reached twenty pounds.

The next few nights my depredations continued. So far my father hadn't noticed, only because I had suddenly volunteered to hoe the squash. Three times a day he went to inspect Mr. K.'s amazing gourds. A yard long, the vines were already developing tiny flower heads. He noticed that the Luperini beetles were all gone, and he wondered what had gotten them. Birds, he guessed. He was wrong.

One night I crossed paths with a deer mouse under the dark canopy of the corn. I'd been seeing them coming and going at a distance, but this one was suddenly in my face. For an instant we stared at each other. I was terrified—all I could think of was hantavirus.

The mouse ran off before I could even move.

I puzzled all the next day how it was that my human awareness, with its dread of hantavirus, had so quickly come to the fore. What did it mean? Could my human thoughts ever win out over the rat?

The impulses of the rat continued to have their way. The rat knew where I'd hidden my sleeping bag in the rimrock. The rat found it, quickly chewed a hole in it, and proceeded to line his nest with down.

Daytimes passed with me working like a dervish in between naps, hoeing, fertilizing, running off the ravens who were as mischievous as ever. Crops didn't have to be ripe to attract their interest; those gluttons would be happy to ruin them anytime.

My father still hadn't noticed what was happening to the squashes. As for the college students, I didn't have to worry about them. They'd taken off on a week's field trip to a farm down in the desert in Arizona that was also growing exotic vegetables for seeds and starting its own catalog. Almost all the late planting was done.

Even though it had been six weeks since it had rained,

all our dry-land crops were holding their own, barely growing while waiting for moisture in order to make their big jump toward putting on size and going to seed.

One day we got some more bad news from the BLM. The ranger drove in and reported that he thought our pothunters were still in the area—that in fact they'd never left. A couple of other sites had been bombed, and maybe some that hadn't been noticed yet. All were on public land, out in the sagebrush country, sites that only a trained archeologist or an experienced pothunter could have detected in the first place.

These guys were making me mad.

As soon as the BLM ranger drove out, my father went out behind the cabin and started smashing cans with his Megamasher, which is an invention of his. I think Duke and Rodney Bishop were making him crazy too. I wanted to help him smash those sleazy cans. I started setting them up as he'd haul on his block-and-tackle, roping that big stone fifteen feet up into the air to the peak of his tripod. It felt good watching the stone fall. The Megamasher may not be the most efficient can smasher ever devised, but it does smash them awfully flat.

Chapter Ten

The day was bound to come, and it didn't take long, when my father noticed. Something had been into the Hopi blue corn, shredding the tiny husks to get at the baby ears inside. "I think it's a rat," he reported one morning at breakfast. "Probably that same one that was in the house. I think he's working the field now."

I felt so ashamed. "Maybe Ringo will get him," I said.

"As long as he isn't coming back in the house, why don't we leave him be?" my mother suggested. "Think what the ravens have done to us. The coyotes get in the corn. . . . Think what a deer has done in one night."

My mother likes to think of us as sharing the valley with all the animals, and so does my father—to a degree. With the exception of deer mice lately, we'd never poisoned anything, and my father didn't even own a gun. When the aphids would get out of hand, he'd order five or ten thousand ladybugs.

"Dusty's good at keeping the deer off," my father replied. "I don't worry about the deer. But it doesn't appear that Dusty's taking care of this rat."

There you're mistaken, I thought. But what I said to my dad was, "This rat is cool! He's got a bushy tail, you know."

My father wagged his head. "A rat is a rat is a rat. And you can bet there's more where he came from. Mama rats, baby rats . . ."

"Maybe not," I countered. "Maybe he's a loner."

My mother got a chuckle out of that. I forged ahead, pleading my case. "Think about all the enemies he has in life. Weasels, skunks, foxes, badgers, coyotes, bobcats, mountain lions, gopher snakes, not to mention Ringo." I was making myself sick with this list. "Owls, too," I added.

My father stopped and stroked his smooth chin. "Tep, I'm surprised. You've always been the best scarecrow I've got. You feel pretty strongly about this rat, don't you?"

"Maybe there's some good that this rat does around here, and we don't even know about it."

My father was interested. "Tell me what you're thinking."

I thought wildly for a line of argument that might

sway him. "Some chili seeds need to pass through the gut of a bird," I began slowly, pausing for a breath and more time to think. "You taught me that. The seed couldn't sprout without the help of the digestive system of the bird."

"Sure thing," my father agreed, proud that I'd remembered.

"Well, rats must help some seeds out, too," I continued. "Maybe in a number of ways. When a packrat moves pinyon nuts around, sometimes he'll drop a nut and pick up something else. Maybe he'll drop that nut in a place where it will sprout and become a pine tree. So he has a valuable place in nature."

"Good point," my father said. "Go on."

"Well, what else . . . Packrats eat insects—I read that in Mom's field guide. For all we know, that rat had a sweet tooth for the Luperini beetles in the gourds. We might lose some squash—corn, I guess you said it was—and a few other things, but the rat might be helping us out in ways you don't even known about!"

My mother was beaming as she put her arm around my shoulder. "That's my boy," she said. "And don't forget, that rat might help make science possible for someone like me forty thousand years from now."

My father couldn't help laughing. "You guys almost have me rooting for the rat!"

"Try to think of him more like a rabbit," my mother

suggested. "He's just as adorable, maybe more so. Rabbits have caused us a lot more grief than packrats."

My dad went out to work and my mother started mixing up some bread dough. Twice a week she bakes outside in the adobe oven my father and I built, and those days are extra special. I watched as she kneaded the bread. She's small, but she has a lot of power in her arms. "Tell me what I was like in the incubator," I said.

My mother looked up, a little surprised.

"No joking around," I said. "I really want to know."

"You fought for every breath," she said. "It would have been so easy for you to just give up."

"How long was I in there?"

"Months."

I snagged a little raw dough, pretending I had to snatch it fast. "How much exactly did I weigh at first?"

"Two and a quarter pounds."

"I really wasn't supposed to live?"

"They told us the chances were ten to one against, maybe worse."

I was standing there wishing she'd say more. Somehow she knew what I was most needing to hear. "You were born with incredible willpower, Tep. You've always had it. You're tenacious about anything worth fighting for. You always have been."

She set the dough to rise. In the heat of a summer morning like this, it would rise quickly. After it rose the first time, she'd punch it down, shape it into loaves, and let it rise again. I went out to get the fire going in the beehive adobe oven. I like to use a combination of scrub oak and juniper. The oak coals burn long and even, and the juniper adds a little flavor. As my fire caught, I was trying to catch fire with the idea that I could control the rat. I had to stop raiding our fields, that's all there was to it. I repeated to myself the words my mother had said: *"You were born with incredible willpower, Tep. You've always had it. You're tenacious about anything worth fighting for. You always have been."*

I can do it, I told myself, if only I'd summon the willpower. No more squashes, no baby corn. None. *None!*

I missed my room. I'd take a little nap there. It was still morning, and the upstairs hadn't heated up yet.

As I woke from my nap, hungry as ever, the delicious smell of fresh-baked bread filled the house. Through the register in the floor, I heard my parents talking about me. "Tep's sleeping a lot," my father was saying. "And he seems to have a lot on his mind."

After a long pause, my mother said, "I think he's just going through a phase."

Right then and there, I decided that I had to take charge of the rat, and tonight would be the night. When I'd accomplished that, I could go back to working on the riddle of what had happened to me. Maybe I could return to Picture House. Maybe I could find that flute.

I took the old fruitcake tin in my hands, and I popped the lid. Here were treasures I couldn't possibly let the rat have: my father's first tepary beans and the ancient corn from Picture House that I would plant soon. For these treasures I would fight the rat with everything in me. If I could prevail, I could start to get my life back. If I lost . . .

I set the lid aside, and I placed the open tin on my desk.

Out of habit, the rat started down for the field that night. I turned him back by picturing the seeds in that fruitcake tin: the little plastic bag of teparies, the bag of corn.

Moments away from the showdown I had staged for myself, I climbed the side of the cabin to Ringo's entry spot, up under the eaves above the second story. Dusty was watching from below. Once inside, I crawled down the rough-hewn log walls and jumped onto my bed. The rat nosed all around the room where the floor met the walls, and then he jumped onto the chair. Now his hands were up on the desk, and he was peering inside the tin.

I could see the seeds now, and so could the rat. In my gut, I could feel the craving. I only wanted to tear at those bags, devour the prize. But from the back of my mind I screamed in my own voice. *"Not those beans! Not that corn!"*

I attacked. I fought with all my willpower, but with a spring the rat was on top of the desk tearing at the seeds. *No!* I screamed, and I fought with everything I had. Not my father's tepary beans. Not my Picture House corn.

Tep! I yelled. *Fight him! Fight for your life, Tep!*

My attack was met by a furious onslaught that shook me through and through with waves of convulsions. I got mad, I kept fighting, I counterattacked. In the end, I beat him. I thrashed him. Now it was the rat that would have to look out through that tiny window, and I could decide what I would and wouldn't do.

I started up the walls toward the hole under the beam, knowing I shouldn't wait any longer before getting back to Dusty. As my bad luck would have it, Ringo appeared suddenly above, making his high-pitched hunting cry like crackling static. He had me trapped and he knew it. How did this happen? I wondered. Where had Dusty been?

The ringtail rushed to the attack. We tumbled across the room, and I fought with teeth and claws as he did the same. He seemed much stronger than the first time we'd met, and I was quickly wearing out—I knew I had to get away. The chance arrived when I bit him on one of his oversized ears. As fast as I could, I scurried up the wall and through the hole next to the beam.

I'd made it outside, but now he had me by the tail. As I swung around to try to get at him, my claws lost their hold on the logs, and I was falling.

It's a long way to the ground from the beams above the second story. I spread my limbs wide to try to slow myself down. The world was flying by and not so slowly. Still, I might have been all right if I hadn't landed with a splash in the rain barrel we keep by the porch.

Chapter Eleven

I came to the surface paddling hard. The rim of the barrel loomed high, high above me. The barrel was less than half full. It hadn't been raining, and this time of the year the only water we had in it was the rinse water from our dishes that we used to water the geraniums around the porch.

Scratch though I might for a hold on the sides of the metal barrel, there was nothing to hold onto and I was tiring fast. The cold was seeping into me and robbing what strength I had.

Slow down, Tep, I told myself. *Don't paddle so hard. Slow down and think!*

I heard something above me and looked up to see the white rings around Ringo's eyes and the white rings on his bushy tail. He was balancing up there, staring down at me. All the while I kept paddling. After some time Ringo disappeared and I saw only an empty circle of dark sky above the pitch-black walls of the barrel.

I was growing more exhausted all the while. Where was Dusty? She was my only chance. But apparently she couldn't hear my frantic squeaks from inside that barrel or hear me scratching on the walls.

Keep paddling, I told myself, just keep paddling. And so I did, far into the night. I thought about my parents, I thought about that word "tenacious" my mother had used, I thought about the long tenacious root of the tepary bean. I drew on everything I had. I wasn't going to give up, I wasn't going to let go. My struggle took me far beyond thinking. Toward the end, it must have been a reflex coming from flesh and bone.

In her search for me, Dusty must have peered at last over the rim of the barrel. At first I felt the barrel being jostled, one, two, three times, and then I managed to look up and dimly recognized the shape of her head above. Again and again, the barrel was rocked as she threw her weight against it, or tried to tip it over with her paws. She couldn't tip it. There must have been just enough water inside that she couldn't manage it no matter how hard she tried.

Dusty rarely barks, but did she ever send up a clamor now, barking like there was no tomorrow. I kept paddling, though my limbs felt like lead.

Suddenly I was blinded by light, and I heard my

father's voice saying, "So what have we here? A nearly drowned rat! It's our bushy-tailed woodrat! I knew you'd come back!"

The blinding beam of his flashlight left me for a second and I was looking up at the silhouette of the enormous head of my father.

Then the light was back on me, blinding me once more. I heard him say, "Your tail's not so cute when it's wet."

Dusty barked again, two, three times. My father hesitated, keeping the light on me but saying nothing.

"He's trying so hard, Dusty," my father said at last. "He's just trying so hard, you have to hand it to him. I wonder how long he's been in there."

Moments later the world turned on its axis as the barrel tipped over and I came flooding out onto the ground. Terrified of what my dad might do, I tried to get up and run away. After taking two or three steps, I keeled over on my side. I was completely spent.

The light blinded me once again. I closed my eyes. I was still gasping for breath. "Good luck, little fellow," I heard my father say. "I hope you revive. You've got a lot of courage." Then the beam of light was gone, and after that the screen door closed.

Dusty reappeared and licked the life back into me, starting my circulation again. In the cool hours approaching dawn, she lay beside me and I snuggled into the warmth of her fur. At last I was able to feel four feet again, and make them work, and I dragged myself back up to the rimrock.

That day I worked closely with my father, and our two rakes sang side by side. Off and on, I found myself starting to sniffle, I was so proud to be his son. He looked at me closely a couple of times that day. I already knew he understood that I "was just going through a phase."

When night came I was determined not to let myself get separated from Dusty again. As for raiding the fields, I was no longer tempted. From now on I would protect them. I owed my father that and more.

It occurred to me that it would be simple enough to hide food during the day that I'd be able to count on during the night. Diced apples covered with peanut butter, a bag of sunflower seeds, whatever I wanted. How could I have been so stupid not to have thought of that before?

I also realized that it might be possible to ride on Dusty's back, where I'd be a lot safer. When night came I tried it out. It was easy, given her long fur, to pull myself up on her back. I knew immediately where I wanted to go, now that I had long-distance transportation. I had to return to Picture House to see if I could find that magic flute.

In place on Dusty's shoulders, I couldn't get her to go straight ahead. She'd walk around in a circle or simply stand still and look back at me. This wasn't going to get us anywhere fast. It was hard for her to catch on to me leading from behind. I realized we needed some kind of a system.

I soon taught her turns with a tug on the left or right ear. Squeaking simply meant "Go!" Before long we'd crossed the road and were headed up and out of the valley. Once she realized we were headed for Picture House, she didn't need directions. No moon lit the way, but that didn't matter: she knew her way by heart.

I started wondering, when the dim outline of the big cave first came in sight, if the BLM ranger still had anyone posted at Picture House. I tasted the night breeze cautiously, and we looked all around. No one was there—except for the packrats, that is, scurrying around on their errands.

Picture House is an eerie place in the dark of the moon. The owl never hooted, but I knew she must still be there, so I clung tight to Dusty's back. It didn't seem there'd been any more digging; I guessed that the pothunters hadn't returned. Had the pueblo elders come for the ancient medicine man and taken him away to hide in a new grave? I made myself go and look, in the room by the picture wall.

The corpse was gone.

I'd come to find the flute that had started all this. Where should I begin?

I knew my mother's rule, that a packrat ranges up to

two hundred feet from its nest. I concluded that the packrat that dropped the matchbook and picked up the flute must have been within two hundred feet of its nest when it took the flute from the albino's fingers. The nest couldn't be very far away.

I looked all around, and had convinced myself there weren't any packrats living close to this end of the ruin. The one who had taken the flute must have been breaking my mother's distance rule, wandering at some distance from home.

But then, as I was double-checking the rubble at the end of the picture wall, a packrat appeared. A single bushy-tailed woodrat. At first I assumed that the rat would be hostile, and I prepared to run. But it approached slowly and, it seemed, peacefully, so I froze, waiting to see what it would do. I was thinking. *This rat might lead me to the flute.* When we were eye to eye, the rat began licking my face and lips. Dusty watched this from a distance. Shuddering, I waited. Suddenly the rat disappeared behind a large rock slab that leaned up against the cliff. I gathered what courage I had. I knew this was my chance; I followed.

Behind the slab was a conglomeration of sticks. The fractures between the rocks were all jammed full of sticks and cactus segments.

I found an entrance. Once inside, I was shaking again. This was crazy. I could never hope to find the flute in all of Picture House! I forced myself forward a little more. I heard nothing. The narrow passage led me deeper into the maze. Then came the drumming of pack-rat feet up ahead, pounding out that warning I'd heard once before. With my supersensitive hearing, it sounded like I was inside a thunderstorm.

The drumming grew even louder as the packrats drew near. Any moment now they'd be on me. Before they even appeared I turned and ran all the way back out and into the open. What chance was there, really, that they had the flute? I didn't want to know badly enough to fight them for the opportunity to find out.

When we returned to the Seed Farm it was still dark, but it was apparent that a change was in the air. A slight breeze first, then a stronger breeze and a rustling in the corn. Dusty, too, was sniffing the air, thick with the promise of moisture.

Very faintly on the warm, moist air came the sound of a very pure instrument, so clean and beautiful it could have been the music of the stars. It was faint yet unmistakable. A flute, that's what it was.

Dusty wasn't perking up her ears. It seemed only I was hearing these notes. I guessed I was only imagining the music of the flute I should have been brave enough to try to recover.

Chapter Twelve

The sunrise that morning was the finest I'd ever seen at the Seed Farm, the finest I may ever see again. I walked down from the rimrock and joined my parents as they watched from the cabin step, hugging each other. A cloud bearing all the colors of the rainbow was advancing on our valley. Out of that cloud, broad shafts of light spoking from the sun lit our world with color from horizon to horizon. My parents reached out and hugged me too, and Dusty made four.

We could hear whooping and hollering from Big Pink, even though it was a quarter mile up the road. They'd never seen the equal of this morning either.

The breeze was out of the south, and it felt all different from the air we were used to, the skin-cracking dry air of New Mexico.

My parents and I were just looking at each other, looking back to the sunrise, feeling about as good as we'd ever felt or were ever going to in this life, I guess. We didn't even try to find words. When a tear left my father's eye, my mother and I couldn't help it either, and then all three of us were sniffling and laughing and shaking our heads. There was more to it than anticipating our crops getting a good soaking, much more than words can tell. I guess rain on its way will do that to you if you're dry-farming in dry country, but this one wrung out our hearts but good.

On the spot, I came within a whisker of telling my secret. I didn't know how much longer I could keep carrying it. Instead I asked, "Did you hear something during the night that sounded like someone playing a flute?"

They shook their heads. "What a lovely thing for you to hear, Tep," my mother said. "I wish I had."

"Oh, probably I was just dreaming."

The moment passed as the looping flight of a magpie caught our attention, winging our way on that tropical breeze. Usually magpies look black and white, but the way the light was glowing this morning, it revealed the blues and purples in the feathers that usually look black.

The bird cocked its head as it flew by, and it cried *"Tepary! Tepary! Tepary!"*

"Maggie!" I called back, but she flew away.

A chorus of ravens brought our attention back around

to the south, to the advancing clouds. Cawing and croaking and cronking, quite a number of ravens were harassing a figure walking up the road, a dark man from the look of him, leaning on a stick—a hunchback, perhaps. Or was he bent into that shape under the bag he was carrying on his back?

"Looking for work, I bet," my father remarked. "Perfect timing—we have some last-minute seed to put into the ground today."

It seems like every summer we'd had at least one illegal alien who came through looking for work. We could never afford to pay them cash to send home to their families in Mexico or Central America, so they usually didn't stay very long. But there was always plenty to eat here if you didn't mind vegetables, and my mother baked extra heavy when the illegals were with us. They'd work for a few days until they got strong enough to continue on. Towns out here are twenty or thirty miles apart, and these men would walk the roads between them without even attempting to hitchhike.

This man, it became apparent as he got closer, was poorer than any we'd met yet. He didn't even have shoes on his feet. He wore baggy trousers and a coarse cotton shirt, obviously homemade, and an ancient straw hat that may have been run over on the road.

As he drew close I was struck by his dark eyes, crackling with intelligence like the eyes of a raven, with maybe a hint of the raven's mischief. It was an Indian face I guess, though he didn't look like he was a Navajo or one of the pueblo people either. From head to toe he was lean as his stick. His skin had the quality of wood, swirling with deeply grooved lines like a burl on a tree, or earth perhaps, dark and cracked by the sun. It was hard to get a fix on his age. Most likely he was very old, but when I looked again, something made me imagine for a moment that he was actually much younger and just looked so old from being out in the weather.

As he eased his sack of possessions from his back to the ground, my eyes went back to his feet, as gnarled as the roots of an old juniper.

"You brought the rain," my father said in greeting.

The man looked behind him at the gathering clouds, and he smiled. His teeth were bad. I wondered if he spoke English.

"You are the Seed Farm?" the traveler asked, with English that sounded like Spanish. His eyes took in all three of us as he said it, not looking at any of us long but acknowledging each of us.

"That's us," my mother said cheerfully. "Art, Lynn, and Tepary Jones."

"Tep-a-ry?"

"That's me," I said. I wondered if he had any idea what my name meant.

To my mother and me, my father said, "Somebody from last summer must have told him about us." And to the old man he said, "We have some seed to plant today."

"That's good."

Dusty was taking a long sniff at the stranger's hand. As she nuzzled it, her eyes rolled up and took in the man's face unguardedly, as if she trusted him at once. It was unusual for her to be so affectionate with strangers.

"What's your name?" my mother asked.

"My name is . . . Cricket."

Now that I look back on it, he never asked for work.

Chapter Thirteen

My job was to get Cricket all lined out while my father was rounding up seed and college students. The clouds were gathering and darkening, and we wanted to get the last late seeds planted before the rain broke.

I grabbed a couple of rakes and stopped to show Cricket the Silver Bullet, where he would stay. As he set his gunnysack inside, I thought I heard beans sliding against each other. That would be a smart food for a poor person to carry, I thought. As my father always said, you could live on beans if you had to. I noticed that Cricket wore something under his shirt. It was suspended from his neck by a cotton string, but I couldn't tell what it was.

The illegals usually recognized a few of our crops from back home. I wondered if Cricket would. "We're going to plant some tepary beans," I told him as we walked into the field. "I was named after them."

"That's good," he said. It was the habit of these men to agree with everything you said. It was their way of getting along in the world.

"We don't have to worry very much about keeping the beans from crossing with each other, because they pollinate themselves."

I was trying to guess if he understood, but his eyes gave no clue. I kept explaining anyway. "With corn we either stagger the plantings or keep the varieties far away from each other—they're pollinated by the wind. The ones that are hardest to keep from cross-pollinating are the melons and squash and other plants that are pollinated by bees. We plant tall plants like corn and amaranth in between the varieties, to block the bees. It makes the bees stick in one patch at a time pretty much."

I was still trying to guess if he was following me. One moment I'd think yes, the next I'd think no.

"That's good," the old man agreed, squinting and looking all around. He appreciated the scope of our gardens, that much was certain. Fifteen acres and four hundred varieties is quite a sight. "What kind of tepary beans you grow?" he asked.

I knew them so well, I could rattle them off. "In the last week or so we've planted black, brown speckled, golden, Morelos white, Hopi white, Kickapoo white,

Mayo white, O'odham brown, Paiute white, Paiute yellow, Pima beige, Pima brown, Pinacate. . . . all these kinds like to get started when it's full summer with long, hot days. The only ones I've got left to plant are the blue speckleds and the Cocopah whites. All it takes now is some rain, and it sure looks like it's coming.''

''You like those tepary beans, eh? Because of your name?''

''Not just that. They don't take very much water, and that's a good thing. A lot of the world doesn't have water to irrigate crops with, and they have a lot of people to feed. With this bean, if you water it very much, it'll make more leaves but fewer beans.''

I started working my rake, preparing a bed for the blue speckleds I was going to start with. The man called Cricket watched me work for a while, and then, I noticed, he bent down and got a little bit of the soil I had prepared, and . . . ate it.

The other rake was lying right there, right beside him, but the old man didn't seem inclined to pick it up and start working. He sat down cross-legged and watched intently as I worked the soil into a finer and finer consistency. I thought this was a good opportunity to show him just how to prepare the soil, so I did an extra nice job. Watching my father work, I'd come to think of a rake as a violin bow. My dad is beautiful to watch as he improvises from hundreds of strokes and shakes of strokes, just like he's making music.

When I was ready I began punching holes in the loam with my finger, planting teparies, patting the soil down on them. "An inch deep and four inches apart," I instructed him. Cricket nodded. It was difficult to tell how much he really understood of what we were doing here. "Some of these varieties," I explained, "were from the last batch that anyone grew *anywhere.* Once people stop growing them, they're gone forever. Seventy-five percent of the food crops that people were growing when Columbus came to America are gone, extinct."

Cricket made a sign across his neck, like he was cutting his throat. I took that to mean he understood, but he could have been agreeing just to be agreeable. He smiled helpfully. It felt a little foolish explaining all this to an Indian, but just because he was an Indian didn't necessarily mean he knew that the old food crops were disappearing from fields all the way from Peru to New Mexico.

He took another little mouthful of soil. It was the strangest thing.

Cricket and I were a good match: I liked to talk, and he liked to listen. "Potatoes came from South America," I continued, really warming up. "When people think of potatoes they think of Ireland, but really potatoes came from the Andes Mountains in South America. Ireland's famous for having a potato famine back in the 1800s. What happened was, there were hundreds of different kinds of potatoes, but they grew only a few. And then a potato fungus got 'em. A million people starved to death. Some of those other kinds of potaotes would've been naturally resistant to that potato fungus."

"Not enough different kinds," Cricket said agreeably.

"The big food companies grow just a few kinds of corn," I said. "Just a few kinds of wheat, a few kinds of everything . . . my father says it's scary. It took thousands of years, millions, for all these different plants to come along, and we think all we need's a few. You can't bring all the others back once they're gone."

"The more the better," Cricket agreed.

"That's right—the more kinds the better. Like with beans. Beans all over the world were having a big problem with a little bug called the Mexican bean weevil. For five years a botanist in South America searched for a kind of bean the weevils wouldn't eat. He couldn't find one. Finally somebody sent him an envelope of ugly little wild beans from Mexico—they weren't even round and smooth like beans. They say he laughed when he saw them. But when he set them in front of the weevils, it was like those beans had some kind of magic armor. It turned out they had a protein that the weevils couldn't stand. The botanists were able to transfer the protein to other beans, including the ones in Africa where people were starving."

"Gotta have enough kinds," Cricket said. "The people who built the pyramids, they didn't have enough kinds."

"The Egyptians?" I wondered.

"The people in the land of always summer."

"Where's that?"

"What you call it—Yucatan, Mexico."

"The Maya people?" I asked.

"Not enough kinds of corn."

"I never heard that before," I said. "That's a good theory."

Cricket picked up one of our Seed Farm packets with the drawing of a Kokopelli petroglyph on the front, playing his flute of coure, and looked at it thoughtfully. "You take a few seeds and make a lot more," he said. "Then people grow them, eh? Do people really do that?"

"Oh, yes, they're growing them all over the place!"

"All kinds of people?"

"Sure! A lot of Indian people are starting to grow them again, plus all kinds of other people. We even got an order from Pakistan this week!"

"That's good," Cricket said softly. "That's very good."

"These seeds aren't going to die out," I said. "We're not going to let 'em."

"That's good, Tepary."

A black-and-white flutter caught my eye, a magpie heading our way. It proceeded to land right on Cricket's shoulder. *"What's to eat?"* Maggie squawked. *"What's to eat? Pass the salsa!"*

I never saw Maggie land on anybody's shoulder before, not even mine. "I'll be," I said.

"You'll be what?" wondered Cricket.

"It's just an expression," I explained.

I marked the blue speckled patch and started raking out another for the Cocopah whites. Cricket got up, bent over, and started planting with his stick, which wasn't a walking stick at all. I'd never seen this before, but I'd heard my father talk about the way the old Indians planted seed. The tool was made of some sort of dense wood, and it had a sharpened point. It was a planting stick.

Now it was time for me to lean on my rake and watch Cricket work. He knelt on one knee as he worked the stick and planted the seed. Maggie was jumping from his shoulder to the ground and trying to get at his seeds, but Cricket's fingers were swift, and he made a game of covering them just before she'd get them.

I looked up, and there at the edge of the field watching the game, with yellow eyes and bushy tail hanging low, was a coyote. The more we get into the summer, the more visits we get from coyotes—they'll eat just about anything. "It's Mister Coyote," I said to Cricket. "I've never seen one come this close while we were working out here. Usually they'll sneak around at night."

Cricket whistled sharply through his teeth and yelled

to the coyote, "You call yourself a hunter! Ha! That's a joke! Where is your tail today? Did you lose it, eh?"

The coyote's head turned, and his eyes seemed to take a glance at his tail. I laughed, and so did Cricket.

"Coy-o-te," he said disparagingly, shaking his head. The coyote trotted off. I told myself to remember that a coyote was making the rounds. Coyotes do like the night, and he'd be back.

The clouds were turning ever darker. The air was stirring thick and heavy, and I could feel the closeness of the rain. I ran back to the house to get my fruitcake tin and my ancient corn from Picture House.

When I got back to the field I showed it to Cricket. "Special corn," I said.

He took a little in his palm, looked at it up close, smelled it. "Haven't seen this kind for a long time," he said.

"No wonder," I said with a laugh. "It's a thousand years old."

I spotted my father hustling by on his own seed run, and I flagged him over. "This is the corn from the seed jar the pothunters dug up," I said. "If these sprout, what are you going to do?"

He had a huge grin on his face. "Turn the Seed Farm over to you!"

"Really?"

"You'd be the master gardener!"

"For how long?"

For a second he hedged, pretending to be considering the possibility of losing. "The rest of this season!"

"I'd be the boss, and you'd do anything I say?"

"You got it!"

"What would yo make him do?" Cricket wondered.

"Make him the Manure Specialist."

In mock horror at the very idea, my dad took off running with those beautiful strides of his, waving the seed packets in his hand, yelling, "Gotta plant this panic grass!"

When the rain started I was slipping the last of my Picture House corn into the earth. I planted it deep, the way the pueblo people still do. Dryland corn needs to have its roots deep where there's always some moisture.

This rain was not a summer take-no-prisoners gullywasher, the kind that can shred crops with three inches of hail. This was a gentle soaker that looked like it might stay a while.

I pitched my tent, but of course I never stayed in it. I was lying awake all night in the body of the rat, listening to the rain on my roof of sticks and bones, wondering what would become of me. It was dry enough inside there, but I didn't think I could bear the loneliness much longer. Before dawn, I heard the mysterious flute music again, pure, clear, and strong, filling up the whole valley. Then I forgot about feeling sorry for myself. My heart went with the music like a leaf down a stream.

The rain continued all day, falling steadily yet softly, supersaturating the ground. I kept waiting for my parents to mention the flute music; surely my mother at least had heard it this time. I began to wonder if I was the only one who was hearing it. In the afternoon I found the college students under their covered porch, watching the rain, chattering, happy to know that all their labor was going to bear fruit. I visited with them for a while until I could test them with the question I'd come to ask.

I figured out a way to ask my question in a round-about way. "Do any of you happen to play the flute?" I asked.

No response. Nothing about the music that had filled the valley.

"How come you asked?" Heidi wondered.

"Oh, I heard some beautiful flute music one time," I said. "I'm looking for someone to teach me."

Chapter Fourteen

The rain continued all night the second night. When a pause came I ventured outside, restless as ever. A brand-new crescent moon was setting in a break in the clouds. I climbed up on Dusty's back and we went down to check on the fields. Everything looked fine until we discovered a coyote in the melons. Dusty's a big dog, and she has no hesitation about chasing a single coyote. That's what she did, and I fell from her back before I could get a good grip.

I hid under a canopy of melon vines until Dusty returned for me. We surveyed the melons, then discovered that the coyote had also been in the squashes and the corn. The coyote hadn't really eaten much of anything; nothing was ripe yet. A nip here and a bite there, just enough to open up a melon or a squash or the corn and ruin them—that was his style.

On our way out of the field, we came across deer mice in my mother's strawberries, at least a dozen of them. Already out of temper, I flew into a rage. We chased them until they disappeared under the greenhouse. The rain started again, and I headed for shelter in the rimrock.

Again, in the hour before dawn, the music of the flute filled the valley.

Again, no one heard it but me.

The first thing I did that morning was check the greenhouse. Ringo didn't have a way into the greenhouse, so if the mice had been getting in there from underneath, in a closed space like that, it could be a bad situation. Hantavirus City.

I opened the door and peeked inside. The windows were all open, and I could feel a steady draft moving through. That was reassuring. With my hand over my nose and mouth I made a tour, looking closely for droppings. The greenhouse looked good and clean.

The rain showed no sign of letting up. Inside the cabin, my mother was baking and my father puttering and singing. They'd declared a holiday for as long as it kept raining.

Mid-morning I put on my rain jacket and went out to see if any of the late-season beans might be sprouting. They'd be the first of our recent plantings to germinate. I knew I was jumping the gun, but I always do. I've always loved to see the way different plants hit the surface. With beans, the seed itself appears out of the ground like the head of a goose tucked up against its long, rising neck, and then the head lifts up and out, splits out, and reveals . . . leaves.

None of the beans had sprouted yet, but the blue speckleds and Cocopah whites were close, the ones Cricket and I had planted only a few days before. I could see the soil lifting slightly where the beans were pushing up from below.

I sensed that someone besides Dusty was there with me. I looked up and found Cricket standing right by me. His clothes were streaming wet and his straw hat was dripping like a sieve. "Those beans—pretty soon now," he said.

"Pretty soon," I muttered, still surprised to see someone standing right there. Dusty was nuzzling his hand. "I've never seen 'em come up this fast," I added. I wanted to know more about this strange old man.

We walked around the fields together. Our feet led us to the chilies, where I thought I'd show off by eating a couple of chiltipines. They're the wild relatives of the chilies people grow. They're tiny, about the size of a wild strawberry. I like them, but they're so hot they'll take your head off. With a glance at Cricket, I ate a couple. As always, it felt like steam was coming out of my ears. Then Cricket ate a handful of them, just like they were berries. "These are good," he said. The chiltipines didn't even make his eyes water or his nose run.

In the afternoon a small blue opening in the clouds widened, and the sun shone through. At once, my mother brought out her fresh bread, and we sat out on the picnic table and enjoyed it, my parents and Cricket and I.

Cricket was saying, "The bread is good," when Ringo dropped out of the low limb of the pinyon there, right onto his shoulder.

My mother was delighted, and my father's mouth was hanging open. The ringtail was so shy, nobody but us had ever laid eyes on him. Even we had never seen him in the daytime before.

Ringo preened on Cricket's shoulder, flicking his flashy tail, Cricket began feeding him bits of bread. A minute later the ringtail vanished back into the trees.

My mother went back inside and returned with a big bowl of fresh strawberries. "Are those washed?" I asked quickly. "I saw some mice in the strawberries."

"I washed them a bunch. They'll be fine."

"I suppose so," I said. All the same, I didn't touch them.

The blue hole in the sky closed with surprising swiftness and the rain began again. Cricket put his hand out and let it fall on his palm. "The female rain," Cricket said. "It's soft, it's good."

The rain fell a third night, soft and steady. I listened for the flute and music came again in the hour before dawn. The rain fell softly all that fourth day, as if it might never stop.

My mother and father spent that afternoon in the rain, completely soaked, holding hands and walking a slow tour among all the different vegetables. I met up with them in the corn we'd planted in the middle of May. It was fully a foot higher than it had been four days before. It looked like it might even tassel soon.

"It's a tropical frenzy!" my father declared.

They were so happy they were giddy. Other than their straw hats, my parents had no protection from the rain and didn't want any. They said they wanted to get soaked, "just like the ground," and they sure accomplished that. It was a warm rain as our rains go, but I think I would have been chilled without my rain jacket. On they went into the beans. Like everything else, the beans had exploded with growth in the last few days. "Holy jumping garbanzos!" my father declared. My mother answered with, "Great leapin' limas!"

I was astonished at the blue speckleds and the Cocopah whites that Cricket and I had planted, the ones that had appeared ready to break through only yesterday. They now stood four inches tall and had already unfolded two sets of leaves. While my parents lingered in the beans, I raced over to the squash, a little apprehensive. The vines were lusher, with much larger leaves, than any we'd grown before. Despite the thinning I'd given them, many young squashes of all sizes and shapes and colors had endured.

I caught up with my parents again in the gourds, where they were visiting with Cricket. Cricket was soaked too, his bare feet caked with mud. My dad was talking about the new gourd vines at their feet. They'd run five feet since I'd seen them only days before, and were in full flower. At the base of the female flowers, striped gourds were swelling, already the size of walnuts. "A botanist we call Mr. K. sent us this seed," my father was explaining to Cricket. "And most of our other seeds as well. I've never seen anything like these gourds. We planted them only a couple of weeks ago!"

Cricket was looking them over. "They're doing good," was all he said, and then he waded into the rest of the gourds, inspecting them carefully. My father followed. It was obvious that Cricket must have some familiarity with gourds. Cricket stopped among the vines of another variety of wild gourd that we were growing for the first time, from a batch we'd planted in early May. "What do you know, one of them's nearly ripe!" my father exclaimed, pointing to a small orange gourd with green stripes.

"Do you know about this gourd?" Cricket asked him.

My father shook his head. He was dying to know whatever it was Cricket knew.

"Did you know it was sweet?"

My father was amazed, and so was my mother. We'd

heard my dad say many times that a wild gourd that just happened to be sweet was probably the ancestor of all squashes and pumpkins.

My dad whipped out his pocket knife, and to my surprise he snipped the gourd from the vine, and bit into it just as Cricket yelled, "Don't do that!" There was a look of shock on my mother's face, but nothing like the shock on my father's. He immediately doubled over with the dry heaves.

It looked like my dad might fall over; my mother steadied him. "Art, are you going to be okay?"

As soon as my dad could quit retching, he spit three or four times, and then he turned to Cricket and said, "I thought you said it was sweet!"

"I said it *was* sweet," Cricket replied. "That was before Coyote grumped on it."

My mother couldn't help it, she burst out laughing. And so did my father, who thought it was the best joke he ever heard. He always did like jokes that were on him.

My mother suddenly felt chilled, and my parents went back to the cabin. Cricket and I went over to the corn to see how it was coming along. My father's sixty-day corn had just sprouted. We weren't the only ones who had noticed. A raven was flying by overhead, looking right down at the new corn. "Here's trouble," I said.

"Oh, yes," Cricket agreed, as the raven flew off with a noisy squawk. "He's already telling the others."

Ravens will go from one corn sprout to the next, pulling them out of the ground. They're so smart, they know that tugging on the leaf will bring up the kernel. "You stay here while I get some things that might scare them away," I told Cricket. It took me a while to round up the poles I'd need, plus parachute cord, a wheelbarrow load of bones, strips from old bedsheets, and other geegaws that would flap in the wind.

On my way back, as I came within sight of Cricket, I noticed a raven just a few feet away from him. Cricket was leaning forward as if talking to the raven. When I got close enough, the huge black bird flew away on thrashing wings. As ravens often do, it gained altitude, then tumbled topsy-turvy with a laughing croak before flying on.

"What were you saying to the raven?" I joked, as I lugged my poles into place. "Making a deal with him?"

"You guessed it," Cricket said with a sparkle in his eye. "Raven hears, raven sees, raven knows, raven decides. I told him if he'd leave this particular farm alone—for good—I'd play a trick on Coyote that would be as good as any that Raven played back in the Distant Time. Raven enjoys getting the best of Coyote."

"Did he go for it?"

"We'll find out, I guess."

The rest of the day, no ravens showed up. I wouldn't have to worry about the ravens pulling out my Picture House corn. It wasn't sprouting.

In the evening the rains finally stopped. The skies cleared with a sunset as remarkable as the sunrise that had begun it all. Even so, the day closed on a worrisome note: my mother had a fever and a cough. "It's just from standing out in the rain all afternoon," she assured my dad. "Make me a pot of rose-hip tea. I'll be fine."

Chapter Fifteen

In the wake of the rains, the night sky blazed with stars. The crescent moon was setting in the western sky. I heard the flute again, this time in the middle of the night. That melody seemed to be calling; I had the feeling it was calling me alone. It made a song of water trickling, the wings of eagles, my parents' voices, the silence of Picture House, wind in the grass, bread baking, plants growing. Dusty and I left the rimrock for the fields below, hoping to find the source of that beautiful music.

The music of the flute was here, there, and everywhere. Finding its source may have been as impossible as arriving at a rainbow's end, but I'd never quit chasing after rainbows either.

We didn't find who was playing the flute but we did

find Cricket, sitting cross-legged in the O'odham squash. His head was tilted back, his straw hat had fallen off. Apparently Cricket had come out to the field to watch the stars, and he'd fallen into a dream or trance. It was very odd. His eyes were rolled back in their sockets so that only the whites were showing. His face looked ancient and still as death in the starlight.

Afraid that the old man had died, I sprung to his knee and leaned against his chest, listening with the packrat's keen ears. I could feel under his shirt whatever thin object hung from his neck by the cotton string. I thought I knew what it was.

His heart beat soundly, with all the power of a drum. He began to speak, though his head was still tilted toward the stars. His eyes remained rolled back in his skull, and his lips never moved. "The stars you call the Milky Way, they are white tepary beans. Coyote scattered them there, making mischief one day."

I had never heard that story before. Of course I liked it.

"My name is Tepary," I told him. "Sometimes I call myself the Human Bean."

Without moving a muscle, the man called Cricket laughed. " 'The Human Bean'—that's a good one!"

I was so amazed he had understood me. I was afraid all he'd heard was the squeaking of a rat.

"It's because of you," Cricket continued, "your mother and father, and others like you, that I stay. Not

115

long ago, I thought the day was coming when there'd be no more use for me. Like the other one, I was close to going.''

"Going where?" I asked.

"To the stars," he replied, and then he fell silent.

I said, "I don't know what you mean."

"But I would miss this world," he continued with a sigh. "Sometimes it's still as beautiful as it ever was. . . . But all things pass eventually, and even my days are numbered."

I didn't think about what I was doing. But I had to tell my secret at last, share my loneliness. I found myself saying, "I'm not really a packrat, you know."

"I know," he said. "You just told me your name was Tepary. I know this Tepary Jones you're talking about. It seems we're both changelings."

I blinked and saw in the old man's place an insect something like a large green grasshopper or locust, maybe more like a katydid. It had large eyes and antennas as long as its body. They were probing in my direction as the insect lifted its wings and began to play beautiful music by vibrating its transparent wing covers so fast they blurred. It sounded exactly like a flute; in fact, it was the same music I'd been hearing all this time. The playing warmed the night and brought back the memory of the warm, moist air that had arrived just before the old man walked up the road and into our lives.

"You are a good flute player," I said.

"Thank you," the insect answered.

"I heard your flute. . . . before you ever got here."

"Yes, you have the hearing of a changeling. You know, I heard someone playing a flute, too, or trying to play it. I came a long way to find out who this new flute player was. I think it must have been you, Tepary Jones."

"It was me," I told the insect. "I tried to play a flute I found, but I didn't really know how to—it wasn't mine. It belonged to a man who's been dead for almost a thousand years."

I went on to explain to the insect how I'd gone up to watch the eclipse of the moon at the ancient ruin we call Picture House, and how the pothunters had come and broken into the medicine man's grave behind the wall.

"What did this medicine man look like? What does this place look like?"

"Well, he was an albino. He had pink skin, light hair. . . . Picture House has five kivas, forty-three rooms, and two towers, and it sits under the roof of a wide cave."

"Ever since I came here, I've been remembering a place close by . . . I think I've been to that place you're talking about, several times. I think I knew this pink-skinned man. The flute you're talking about didn't belong to him either. It was passed down from the Distant Time.''

''How could you have . . . do you mean . . . did the flute belong to the humpbacked flute player himself? Did it belong to Kokopelli?''

''One of them.''

''There was more than one Kokopelli?''

''There were two.''

''You said, 'One has gone.' Is that what you meant? Kokopelli has gone?''

''Yes, and one remains.''

Before I could put into words what I was thinking, the insect said, ''Now let me guess, you tried to play this flute . . .''

''I didn't really play it, I only blew on it a little.''

''That's all it took! That's how you became a magical person! You see, with that flute, you can change into an animal or back to a person. That's its magic. That flute goes back to the very earliest days, when people and animals traded places all the time.''

''Why do I keep changing back and forth every day and every night?''

''Did you play the flute during the eclipse?''

''Yes, exactly when the moon was blacked out.''

''Then that must be why.''

''Well, I lost that flute!''

''That's too bad! That was some flute!''

With that, the large green insect was gone, and the

old man we called Cricket was back, his eyes still rolled back in his skull.

"Cricket," I asked, "You still have your flute, don't you? Is that a flute you keep under your shirt?"

He drew it out and showed it to me. It was identical to the bone flute I had lost. "Is it made from the wing-bone of an eagle?" I asked.

"Yes, Eagle gave it to me," he replied.

"May I . . . may I have your permission to say your name?"

"Certainly."

I tried to speak, but the word wouldn't come out. My heart was beating so fast I couldn't even breathe. "It's hard for me to say it!" I blurted out.

He laughed.

I took a deep breath, then tried again. "You are . . . *Kokopelli.*"

The old man's ancient eyes glinted with the starlight of the eons. "There, you said it! I'm one of two. . . . yes, 'Kokopelli' is what the People always called me."

"You are old. . . ."

"Very old."

"Thousands of years old?"

"Thousands."

"And you came to see us. . . . are you by chance Mr. K., too—the one who's been sending us seeds all this time?"

"Sure, that's me."

"I wish I could tell my parents all about you! They love Kokopelli, and they love Mr. K."

"I know. But you can't tell them anything more than what they can figure out for themselves. Magical persons have secrets no one else can understand."

"Can you help me, Cricket? Can I still call you Cricket?"

He chuckled and said, "Call me Cricket. Yes, I'll help you if I can. But you don't seem like you need any help."

"But every night I'm in the body of this woodrat."

"The woodrat people are good people."

"My mother likes woodrats," I told him.

"She is an unusual person. Is it a secret, what your mother studies in the basement?"

I told him about my mother studying the midden at the ruin where I had found the flute, and the middens two and four and six miles away. He liked the idea that she could send away samples and find what century they came from.

"She loves the ancient times, the ancient people," I said. "She's trying to find out why they left."

Cricket heaved a sigh. "Time will have its way—everything that flowers, dies. Yet it can also live on in a new way, as long as the seeds are good. You know these things."

At that, Cricket took up his flute and played his song

120

of wind and rain and stars, the same song the insect had played with its wings.

The path of Dusty's eyes caught my attention. I noticed that she was following the advance of a squash runner that was moving up Cricket's leg and over the top of his knee as he played, climbing toward the flute. I was watching its leaves, tendrils, and flowers opening before my very eyes.

Cricket took the flute from his lips. "Tell me how your father first came to love the seeds."

"He grew up in a city—Chicago. His parents grew up in Chicago, too. It was his mother's parents who used to live on a farm, somewhere in the middle of Ohio. My father never used to know much about the farm, but when he was about my age he came across an old fruitcake tin among his mother's things in the basement, and in that fruitcake tin, along with other mementos of her mother, he found a handful of beans in a small jewelry box."

"That's good," Cricket said.

The squash, I noticed, had slowed considerably since Cricket had left off playing, yet my eyes could still detect motion as I continued with my story: "My father asked his mother about the beans, and his mother told him that her family had always grown these beans in their vegetable garden on the farm, over many generations, for a hundred years or so. According to the story that was passed down with the beans, the first of her family to come into that country were starving early in their first winter. It had been a terrible fall, with one blizzard after another, and the family had nearly run out of food. The nearest settlement was sixty miles away. They knew they wouldn't make it until spring.''

''That's very bad,'' Cricket said.

''They were saved by an Indian family who'd had their land taken away from them. The family was moving west, to try to join some relatives. The Indian family gave my father's great-great-great grandparents enough beans to get them through the winter. Ever since then, my father's ancestors kept those beans going, as a way of remembering, and because they were good beans, too.''

''Sure, sure.''

''But when my grandparents left the farm, nobody kept raising the beans. The last ones were in the fruit-cake tin.''

''That's very bad.''

''I know. My father tried to plant some of them, but of course they wouldn't sprout. That's when he first started to learn about seeds, how you have to keep them going. It took a long time, but finally he found a way to start the Seed Farm and keep other kinds of beans going, and lots of other things, too.''

''That's a good story. Your father is a good person.''

''I know. Now there's something I want to ask

you . . . can your flute make it stop happening, make me stop turning into a packrat?''

"Oh, no, my flute can't do that. My flute brings rain, makes things grow. And it might have some healing power still.''

I was thinking hard. "If I got the other flute back, what would happen if I blew on it again?''

"I'm not sure you should do that. You might turn into a snake, or a spider, or a bear or something. That's a powerful flute. You have to know the right notes to erase what you did before. I don't think you can simply blow on it again. You should think about staying how you are—a human being and a rat. You've been lucky.''

"Lucky!''

"It's an opportunity other people will never have.''

I paused and thought about what he had said, but still it didn't seem like an opportunity to me. "Will I have to wait for the next eclipse of the moon?''

"That won't be very long from now. . . . sixteen years.''

"Sixteen years! I'd be twenty-nine years old!''

"You wouldn't have to wait if you knew the right notes. If you knew the right notes, and you had the flute, you could undo this anytime.''

"What are the right notes?''

"The problem is, that flute wasn't mine to begin with. The pink-skinned man would know the right notes—he was the last one to inherit that flute and know its secrets.

With the power of that flute, he could change into different animals and back to himself. This man you're talking about, he made some of the pictures up there where the people lived in the cliff. He told me he was going to leave a message in the pictures about a few very important notes for that flute.''

"Which pictures have that message?"

"Describe them for me—maybe I'll remember."

I described the lightning, the bird-headed men, the bear tracks and the rest. He stopped me when I described the two spirals surrounded by corn, with the flute players on either side.

"Spirals?" he asked.

I drew a spiral in the dirt, starting in the center and then making tight circles growing out and out.

"Sure, I know what you mean. Those are the pictures he was making. Sometimes those spirals show the people's journeys between worlds and their migrations in this world. I have a feeling those pictures tell the notes you want to know, but it wasn't something for me to know myself. It's not my flute.''

"Thank you anyway," I said. "Maybe that will help."

"Will you help me with something?"

"Sure. What is it?"

"Raven's waiting for us to play that trick on Coyote. Coyote's been causing trouble in your field, you know."

"I know."

"If we can trick Coyote, you won't have any trouble from either one of them again. Coyote's over there in the corn right now. That's where you'll meet him, and then you lead him to the gourds."

"Can Dusty come with me?"

"Of course you can't take Dusty with you—Coyote would never go for that. You'll have to be alone. In the gourds, that's where we're going to play a little trick on him. I want you to get Coyote into a gourd-eating contest. Coyote loves to gamble. Make him promise that if you win, he'll leave your fields alone forever. Then so will Raven."

"I'm going to eat a *gourd*?"

"The gourd *you* eat will be from a special seed I brought from Mexico. I planted it four days ago and I've been giving it special attention. The special gourd seed is from a vine I found growing in the dry shadow of the mountains down there—the only one of its kind."

"But how can I eat a gourd? Look what happened to my father!"

The old man said mysteriously, "Look for a sign, and believe that you can do it. You are Tepary Jones!"

"But what if Coyote wins?"

Cricket thought about it, and then admitted with a shrug, "I guess he eats you."

Chapter Sixteen

I left Dusty with Cricket and made my way toward the Hopi corn. I hardly had an idea what I was supposed to be doing. The breeze stirring my whiskers seemed to carry a warning, but I couldn't tell what was wrong. My heart was beating out of control. Without Dusty I was an easy target for all the night hunters. I paused, thinking I could hear the slightest bit of movement.

Then I saw it—the tail end of one of our enormous gopher snakes disappearing down a hole.

In a moment, the snake had vanished. I held my breath and kept on moving. Up ahead, I could hear something the likes of which I'd never heard before. Using the cover, I crept toward the sound and found it was coming from a small patch of Hopi blue corn—the ears were not only ripe, they were bursting from their husks! Hopi corn grows in squat bunches, never getting very tall at all, but these plants were reaching the height of a grown man right before my eyes!

The sound of the corn had attracted someone else. I saw the eyes first, intelligent and mischievous, glowing in the dark. They were the yellow eyes of Coyote, and they were locked on me. His tall ears were perked forward—I knew he'd make a dash for me at any moment.

Running couldn't help me; it was too late for that. I had to do something to throw him off, something strange. Somehow a tip beetle's antics came to mind, and I did exactly what the tip beetle does: I stuck my head under the dirt and kicked my hind feet up in the air.

I could see nothing now, but I held that position for it seemed like forever, until I heard Coyote's voice above me. "Ho, Rat, I'm going to bite you."

"Hold on there," I said.

"What's that you said? Speak clearly!"

I was madly trying to think, to think of anything. "Hold on!" I hollered. "I hear something strange down here!"

"Oh, yeah? What is it?"

"Quiet, I'm listening to the people down here. They're saying something about you."

I heard Coyote digging, and I counted to twenty. Then I pulled my head out of the ground and saw, just as I'd hoped, that his head was under the soil. I started to run away but he was too quick for me. With a glance over my shoulder, I saw him sailing through the air with an arching leap. Now he had me in his jaws.

I knew that he would want to play with me a little, as coyotes do, before he shook me hard and broke my neck. And that's what he did. He stood on two legs and tossed me high in the air. I was still in the air when something else caught his attention—the sound of bursting ears of corn, louder than before. "Listen to that corn!" Coyote marveled as I hit the ground.

My mind was racing. Only with more strangeness, I thought, could I keep Coyote distracted. All I could think of was to say, "What is corn?" as innocently as if I was born yesterday.

Coyote tossed his long snout into the air and laughed. " 'What is corn?' " he howled. " 'What is corn?' Ha-ha-ho, hee-ha-ho-hee! 'What is corn?' "

Even as we spoke, the husks were opening and enticing Coyote with rows of blue corn.

" 'What is corn?' " Coyote asked with a smirk, as he took an ear and made short work of it. "This is corn, O Rat!"

The juicy kernels made foam around Coyote's mouth as he ate one ear after the next. In between gulps, he said, "You have got to be the stupidest rat I've ever met! Ever even heard of! Why, corn is plump and corn is delicious, corn is blue and corn is golden, corn is red and corn is sweet and corn is practically better than . . . *meat*!''

Coyote tore into every ear from that little patch, eating only a mouthful from each and dropping it on the ground before he greedily started in on the next.

I told him, ''I used to eat that stuff you call corn. But it just doesn't compare. . . .''

Coyote's ears stood up sharply, and his huge tail switched back and forth. ''Compare to what?''

''Follow me,'' I said. ''I'll show you something that will make your taste buds forget all about this stuff.''

When I led him to the gourds, Coyote's yellow eyes flashed angrily. ''You are definitely the stupidest rat I've ever laid eyes on! You think you can fool me with one of these?''

With a backward glance, I saw Coyote's teeth clicking, and there was murder in his eye. I kept moving through the gourds, looking for the one I was supposed to eat. How was I supposed to tell? Cricket, I thought, I'm in big trouble now. ''Look for a sign,'' you said. I don't see any sign!

All around the gourd patch I scurried, concentrating as best I might, looking for a sign, but I couldn't think with my heart in my throat. Closer and closer behind me came the sound of Coyote's snapping jaws. I was about to run for my life when something moving caught my eye: the katydid's long green antennas, seeming to wave me toward him. The insect was perched on top

129

of a striped gourd. That must be the one I needed! As soon as I got there, the insect was suddenly gone. Quickly I bit through the stem fastening that gourd to its vine, and turned with the gourd in both hands to face Coyote. "Much sweeter than corn," I said confidently.

Coyote was grinning. "Sure it is, Rat. Go ahead and eat it. Prove how sweet it is. You eat one, and then I'll eat one."

"Gladly," I said. "But let's make it interesting. If I eat mine, every bit, but you don't eat yours, every bit, then this whole field is mine and you can never come back."

"Yes, of course," Coyote said. "I want to see this."

It was my moment of truth. Cricket said I could eat this gourd. It was crazy, but I trusted him, that old man, that bug, Cricket, Mr. K., Kokopelli.

Boldly, I bit into the gourd. It was sweet like a sweet squash, almost like a melon. From a vine he'd found in Mexico, Cricket had said, one of a kind. I chewed noisily and happily, smiling all the while. My father would be amazed! A wild gourd in Mexico, from its treasure house of hidden genes, had thrown a sweet mutant, just like its ancestor that had started the squashes! This gourd tasted sweet as a peach! Smacking my lips, I finished it off, enjoying Coyote's astonishment.

Fortunately, with all the vines crisscrossing each other, Coyote didn't happen to pick a gourd from the same plant. He bit into his as enthusiastically as I had mine, but his mouth suddenly puckered and he was spitting out the pieces. "Ugh! Ah! Ooh—awful! Disgusting!"

"Remember," I admonished him, "you have to eat the whole thing, or give up this field."

"I'll gladly give up this field, O Rat!" With that, Coyote trotted off, his tail hanging even lower than usual.

When he got to the edge of the field, Coyote paused and looked back at me. "Some other time, Rat," he said. "Some other place." He shook his head back and forth, and he coughed and spit. At that he turned and ran briskly into the night. Just then I heard the laughing of ravens.

When I hurried back to report my success to Cricket, I found Dusty in the squashes, right where I left her, but Cricket was gone. Dusty whined and tapped her old tail, grateful to see me. She looked up to see the headlights of a truck that was slowing along the road.

Dusty had to go investigate. Trucks hardly ever came through the valley in the middle of the night, and why was this one slowing, stopping?

I was right behind her, in the panic grass, when the spotlight fell on her. Poachers trying to spotlight deer? Dusty walked a little closer, blinded by the light.

A shot was fired. It sounded strange, not like a pistol or a rifle—more like a pellet gun. Dusty stood still at

131

first, as if nothing had happened. Then she wobbled, and then she collapsed.

There was a tranquilizer dart sticking out of her side.

The spotlight went out. Two men jumped from the pickup and ran over to Dusty and grabbed her up. I was right there, in the panic grass, but they didn't see me. One had a beard, the other a drooping mustache.

The pothunters!

"Nothing like the right tool for the job," snickered the squat man with the beard. "A pot-sniffing dog!"

The pothunters threw some blankets around Dusty and placed her in the back of the pickup. Then they got in the front and fired up the motor. There was no way I was going to watch them drive away. I leaped onto the back bumper, but I couldn't claw my way up and over the tailgate.

The truck was starting to move. I jumped free and ran forward underneath it, looking for a place to stow away.

I was running at full speed under the engine compartment, with the truck accelerating fast, when I jumped onto the frame, then climbed up the side of the motor and clung to the ignition wires feeding into the distributor cap.

It was a long and bumpy ride, and I suffered from the heat of the motor. We were climbing, I could tell that from the sound of the gears. I had time to begin to add up what had happened. Someone must have talked about Dusty.

I could make a pretty good guess. Our college students would have talked about Dusty in town, at the laundromat or at the café, about her finding the pot in front of Big Pink. Probably they'd passed on the history of her glorious archeological career that I should have kept to myself. Talking wouldn't have hurt a thing, if the pothunters hadn't still been around to hear about it.

That's all it had taken.

Chapter Seventeen

At last the truck lurched to a stop. I heard the truck doors slam, and then the tailgate go down. One of the men said, "Let's put her over by that tree."

I scurried out, relieved to get away from the hellish heat of the motor. From behind the front tire I watched them laying Dusty down. She was still unconscious.

I could smell where I was even before I saw the shapes of the big trees in the starlight. I was up on top of Enchanted Mesa, where the yellow pines grow, the stately ponderosas with jigsaw-puzzle bark that smells like vanilla. I knew exactly where on the mesa I was. This was the one stand of old tress the loggers hadn't gotten to yet.

The pothunters tied Dusty to the tree, and then they took a couple of black-on-white pots out of the pickup's toolbox behind the cab. The brother with the mustache walked off with the pots, and the one with the black beard disappeared inside their big sheepherder tent.

I followed the one with the pots, taking advantage of what little cover the forest floor offered. He was heading toward a cluster of boulders shielded by a thicket of scrub oak.

As soon as he'd hid the pots and turned back toward his camp, I investigated. I found four big water jars, several seed jars, half a dozen wide bowls, an effigy pot in the shape of a parrot, and mugs with lizard, wolf, and bird handles. All were beautifully painted with intricate black-on-white designs.

Where was the basket with the medicine man's bundle? I searched all around the big rocks. It wasn't to be found. Then I realized that the seed jar I'd seen them with at Picture House, the one my ancient corn came from, wasn't here either.

Where were they?

I hastened back to their camp, determined to make the most of the time I had left until dawn caught me.

My first instinct was to chew the rope that held Dusty, and so I did, close to her collar, just in case she'd wake up and we could escape together. I quit just before chewing the rope all the way through, so it would look like she was still tied. Dusty wasn't showing any signs of stirring yet. I listened for her heartbeat. It was slow, but it was there. How long would it take for the drug to wear off?

Next I peeked into the men's tent. They were sleeping on cots, both already snoring. I looked all around under the cots for stolen artifacts, but I didn't find any. The thick bed of pine needles made a nicer floor than the Bishop brothers deserved. I found a box of ammunition and their smelly boots. Of course they wouldn't leave artifacts right in their camp. And they wouldn't load up their plunder from its hiding place until the moment they were going to leave the area.

Their leather boots seemed too tempting. I chewed some pretty good-sized holes in them. I even chewed their bootlaces through in a number of places.

Where were their keys? I could keep them from going anywhere!

I held my breath, came out into the open between the cots, and took a good look. On top of a milk crate they'd turned upside-down between the heads of the cots, next to a billfold and a gun belt, there it was—their key ring.

Tiptoeing to the crate, I stood on my hind legs and came to eye-level with the key ring. The problem was, the bearded brother had his face practically in the keys.

He smelled bad, like chewing tobacco.

When I tried to take the key ring in my mouth, my whiskers touched his beard, and his hand came to his face like he was swatting at a bug.

I darted beneath his cot and waited. Before long he was snoring again.

I got set to try again. He'd moved a little and made it even harder. He was breathing right on me. That breath could have corroded metal. This time, just as my teeth were about to close on the key ring, my whiskers got inside his nostrils. He grunted and slapped himself in the face. Again I darted away under the cot.

When my heart slowed, I looked again. The first hint of dawn was starting to show. I had to make the most of the time I had left.

Then I realized, Forget about the keys! They might have a second set anyway!

I raced out of there and under the truck, climbed up onto the motor and started chewing wires as fast as I could. All the wires I could reach, I chewed them up and chewed sections out of them so they wouldn't be able to splice them back together. Then I hid the pieces in a patch of scrub oak.

Something about those shiny keys, though—I couldn't resist them. I scurried back into the tent. The sun would rise in a few minutes. I thought I had time. . . .

Fortunately, the ugly man had turned over. I was free of him and his face and his breath. This time I took the keys in my mouth. They jingled slightly. Ever so carefully, I made my way out of the tent and started into the nearest trees, where I buried them under the pine needles.

From a scrub oak thicket I kept watch on Dusty. The sun rose, I underwent my transformation, and still she hadn't moved. A raven flew close, and I could see its dark, intelligent eye looking right at me, almost through me. What did the raven know? What had Cricket called me, a "changeling"? That I was.

I had a bad feeling about my mother. She'd gone to bed with a fever and a cough. Isn't that the way it begins with hantavirus? I had to get to her as fast as I could, and yet I couldn't leave Dusty behind.

As the sun climbed ever higher in the morning sky, I was growing more and more desperate, certain my mother was sick. Time slowed down, almost stopped. Seconds hung suspended, like slowly dripping water. At last Dusty began to twitch and shake, and finally she lifted her head. With great effort she rose on wobbly legs. I was about to go to her when the bearded brother appeared at the front of the tent, holding his chewed boots in his hands. The man looked at Dusty, a long look. I held my breath. He turned barefoot to making a fire and starting coffee. He hadn't noticed the fray on the rope near her collar.

His brother appeared, the tall one with the mustache, and they both were cussing about whatever varmint had chewed up their boots.

"Left a pine cone in place of the keys," said the bearded man. "Had to be a packrat."

Dusty was starting to look okay.

Mustache sat on a log and pulled on a pair of socks, then pulled his boots on. The socks showed through in two or three places. "This is stupid," he said, as he began to knot the laces back together.

"One more night. I want to see what this pot-sniffing dog can do. Then we're heading home."

I thought, There's no chance Dusty would dig for you. But what would they do to her when she wouldn't?

"Yeah, well, Duke," the tall one said slowly. "I just don't like that place. Why don't we just pick up that medicine bundle and that pot we cached there and call it good?"

"Superstitious, eh?"

"You've got to admit things were more than a little strange—the ball of fire and all. *You* explain it."

"Don't care what it was, Rodney. Shut up and make some breakfast so we can eat something and go back to sleep. How 'bout steak and eggs?"

I had to listen to them for another hour. They never said anything else that was important. Cuss and spit and rail against the government, that's all they did. At last they went back to their cots. They hadn't discovered about their truck yet.

I thought I was in the clear when I tiptoed to Dusty. I was just slipping my hand into my pocket for my pocket knife when the one with the mustache—Rodney—appeared at the front of the tent, in his skivvies and bare feet, and saw me there with Dusty clear as day, not twenty feet away. He yelled at the top of his lungs, "Duke! There's a kid out here!" then came sprinting at me.

Eleven years old Dusty was, and meek as a lamb. I'd never even seen her curl her lip in all that time. I thought that guy had me dead to rights, when Dusty came snarling between us, vicious as a pit bull, and bit him bad on the hand.

I'd heard the pop of the rope as she lunged; she was free.

Holding his hurt hand, Rodney backed off. Duke was at the front of the tent taking all this in. Now he turned quickly back inside.

"Dusty!" I yelled and took off running. She was right with me. I tore into the cover of the nearest scrub oak and we plunged down the side of the mesa together.

Behind us came gunshots, loud as cannons. But with all this brush, I knew they couldn't see what they were shooting at.

After a few minutes I slowed down to a jog. I had a long way to run. We wouldn't have to worry about them chasing us, not in those boots of theirs.

Nine miles cross-country and we'd be home.

Chapter Eighteen

All the days of my life led up to this one. As I came running up to the cabin my father stepped outside. He looked so scared he didn't even ask me where I'd been. "Your mother . . ." he managed. "She's much worse than when she went to bed last night."

I found my mom in the living room, where my father had set her up in the hide-a-bed. She was propped up on her pillows, absorbed in the view through the windows onto the fields. Her face was flushed with fever. I was sure she had hantavirus, and I was sure she'd somehow caught it from me.

My mother's face lit up when she saw me. I had to fight to keep from crying. "Hey now, Tep," she said with a smile, "Where have you been this morning? You're all scratched up."

"All over the place," I told her. I'd intended to tell her and my dad about the pothunters; I'd intended to call the sheriff and the BLM ranger. Now all of that would have to wait. I wasn't going to get anything stirred up right now that might involve my parents. Those pothunters were good and stranded. My mother was too worn down, and my father was too worried about her, for either of them to be worrying about me.

"You should go to the hospital," I told my mom.

She took my hand as I knelt by her side. "I'm fine," she assured me. "Your father and I already talked about that. Tep, really I don't feel that bad. I just caught the flu from being silly and standing out in the rain."

"*Lynn,*" my father said, "you're just so *stubborn.*" He turned to me and threw up his hands. "She's got a cough, muscle aches, a headache, fever: all the early symptoms of hantavirus."

"The symptoms of the flu," my mother maintained. "I'm going to stay home where I can get well."

My father shook his head, but said nothing further. He turned and went into the kitchen.

My mother pressed both my hands in hers and met my eyes. "Even if it is hantavirus, Tep, I've decided against going to the hospital. You know how people are dying on the way, or once they get there—"

"Don't even talk like that!" I pleaded. "Don't—"

"Listen, Tep. I'd stand more to lose on the way to the hospital than what I'd gain by getting there. I've

142

thought about it, quite a lot. If it's hantavirus, my best chance is right here, on the Seed Farm, with you guys. You guys and the Seed Farm are my strength. I'll need every bit of my strength, if that's what it turns out to be.''

"But, Mom—"

''Take me away from here, jostle me around, and my roots would go into shock.''

She managed a smile. I couldn't. My father returned with a small bag of ice cubes which he wrapped in a washcloth and pressed against her forehead.

The minutes passed, long as hours. My mother drank a cup of echinacea tea, which is supposed to be good for the immune system. Then she closed her eyes, fighting her battle. She looked so calm. I knew my father was anything but calm. He couldn't go against her wishes, yet he knew he was losing the chance to call for help.

It seemed to me, as the hours ticked away, that she was worsening. My father kept changing the icepack on her forehead to cool her down, but her fever was worse and her breathing was becoming more and more labored. At one point she opened her eyes and asked my father, ''Do you hear that flute?''

My father was startled. ''No . . . Do you hear a flute?''

''It's coming from on top of the bookcase,'' she said.

My father and I stood and went to the bookcase. On

top of a stack of scientific journals was the large green insect I'd met in the night, vibrating its wings as before. I wondered why I couldn't hear the music now. The insect was exactly the same: bright green, with huge eyes and long, waving antennas. I remembered how the old man, his eyes rolled back in his skull, had changed into this insect and back again.

"Tep, can you hear the music?" my mother asked.

"He's playing just for you," I replied.

My dad said, "There's only some kind of katydid over here, Lynn. We don't hear a flute. It must be your fever. I wonder what species this is. I've never seen one exactly like it before."

My mother sighed. "Really, I do hear it. It's the most beautiful music I've ever heard. It sounds something like water, and something like the wind, and a lot of other things—everything that's beautiful, Tepary. It's indescribably beautiful, and very soothing."

My father looked more worried than ever. "Don't get mystical on us, Lynn."

With a slight smile, my mother said, "There's more on heaven and earth than is dreamt of in our philosophy."

"You're tired," my father insisted. "You should rest."

"Yes, I think I'll try to sleep." She motioned toward the teacup on her nightstand. "After a while, I'll have another cup of echinacea."

My dad went out to brew some more tea. I kept watch by my mother. She nodded off.

I went to the dresser and whispered, "Thank you, magical person, for playing for my mother."

The insect didn't answer, but kept on playing, trilling its transparent wing covers.

When my mother woke, late in the afternoon, she told us she felt better though she looked even worse to me. Then she announced, "I want to tell you what I've learned from my midden studies."

"You shouldn't try," my father said firmly. "It'll take too much out of you."

"I still think it's the flu. Now listen."

My father bit his lip as my mother drew herself up in the bed, gathered her strength, and said, "I've made some conclusions."

"You don't have to tell us," my father insisted. "Not now."

"But I've been waiting so long to tell you, both of you. Now listen! This is important to me!"

My father took her hand. "I'm sorry," he said.

"This is what the packrats tell us: when the people first built pithouses in the cave, two thousand years ago, tall trees grew close by, ponderosa pines like we find up on Enchanted Mesa today. The Enchanted Mesa ponderosas are only a remnant."

"That's remarkable," my father said.

"Yes, it is. And the big trees didn't grow only around

Picture House. At all three other midden sites it was the same story. During the twelve hundred years people lived here, I found a gradual decline in the evidence of ponderosas in the rat middens. A hundred years before the abandonment there was none at all. No needles, no seeds, no ponderosa bark flakes, no cone segments . . ."

"The people cut down all the trees?" I wondered.

My mother rested and then she said, "They might have used them up, every one. When their tall pine forest was gone, the subsoil in their fields would have dried up, less rain and snow would have fallen. . . ."

My father whistled softly. "The big drought came, they couldn't raise nearly as much food. . . ."

"Their populations would have crashed, and the survivors moved on."

My mother waited, closed her eyes, then spoke again. "People dried up other places by cutting down their trees. . . . Greece and Turkey . . . Lebanon . . . Morocco . . . lots of places. It's going on today more than ever, all over the world. We can learn from the story the packrats tell about Picture House."

"What a hypothesis," my father said.

"That's all it is—my Packrat Hypothesis. If we do the same studies at Chaco Canyon and Mesa Verde and a lot of the other sites, it would be very exciting to compare our findings. Maybe those places were deforested, too. It might only be one piece of the puzzle of their disappearance and the migrations of the pueblo ancestors, but it might be an important piece."

At that, my mother started coughing violently, wheezing for breath. Her face turned beet red. My father was greatly alarmed, and so was I. When she could manage it, she drank some water. I ran for new ice for her forehead.

"Now you need to rest," my father was saying when I returned.

My mom shook her head, and said with a smile, "I guess I know too much about time. I know how precious it is."

She was much worse, it was obvious.

My mother closed her eyes, calmed herself. A few minutes later she made the little clucking sound she's always used for Dusty, and Dusty got up and stood by the bed. "What happened to the flute music?" she asked suddenly. "It's gone."

I looked over to the top of the bookcase. "So is the katydid."

Just then came a soft knock at the door. "Come in," my father said.

The old man removed his beat-up straw hat and walked in. He was stooped over, barefoot as always, as weather-beaten as mud that has cracked and dried in the sun.

My mother opened her eyes wide and greeted him with a smile. "It's good to see you, Cricket."

My mother laid her hand on the broad crown of Dusty's grizzled head. "Good girl," she said, and then my mother looked up at my dad and me, and said sheepishly, "I have a confession to make."

My father said, "Lynn, what are you talking about?"

It was getting so much more difficult for her to speak. She hardly had the breath for it. "I've been hoping . . . it was only the flu. I'd convinced myself it was only the flu. Suddenly I'm not so sure. I should tell you this. I cleaned out the greenhouse about ten days ago."

I already understood, but my father was completely confused. "What do you mean?" he asked her.

"My packrat studies didn't make me sick. I discovered . . . the deer mice had gotten into the greenhouse—quite a few of them."

My father went pale.

"I know, I know," my mother said. "I thought I was being so careful. I opened the windows, wore my mask. . . . I guess the virus is a lot finer than the mesh on my mask."

My father put his head in his hands. My mother reached for him and put her hand on his cheek. "I didn't want one of you guys beating me to it. I just should've left the greenhouse alone. I found where the mice were getting in . . . I plugged it up. It shouldn't be a problem again."

"Lynn," my father said gravely. "If this goes much

148

further, your lungs will suddenly start to fill with fluid. Maybe they already are."

"Please, Art," she said. "Don't start that again. I know where I should make my stand."

Cricket's ancient eyes were suddenly lit with an idea. He turned to me and said, "You spoke of the pink-skinned man's medicine bundle. Tell me, Tepary, did it have any plants in it—herbs?"

"Some roots."

"Anything else?"

"Well, there were a lot of little pouches. I don't know what was in them."

"Herbs would be in a few of them. There might be something in the pouches that would help your mother. The people in those days, they used to get this same sickness that keeps you from breathing."

My father's mind was racing. "Is it an herb that we'd have around here? Maybe we grow it on the farm!"

Cricket shook his head. "It's all gone. People stopped growing it."

I could barely speak, I was so struck by the old man's words. I was remembering something the pothunters had said. I blurted out, "I think they hid the medicine man's basket up around Picture House!"

My father didn't even stop to ask me why I thought this was true. He could see I was pretty certain.

My mother suddenly sat up straight and looked at Cricket, as if for the first time. "I just figured it out.

149

You know too much about plants to be just anybody. *You* are Mr. K.! You've come to see us at last!''

Cricket nodded, and then said, "Yes, I've come to visit at last.''

My dad was taken completely by surprise. He looked at my mother, then back at me. "Cricket is Mr. K.!''

"I've gotta hurry,'' I said, heading for the door. "I've got to get to Picture House.''

My father's eyes blazed with fear and hope. "Run like a deer, Tep!''

My mother motioned me back with the wave of a finger. She had me lean close, and then she kissed me on the cheek. With a whisper, she said, "I'll be here, Tepary.''

Chapter Nineteen

The sun was dropping fast. With Dusty at my side, I ran. I ran with my heart in my throat, terrified that my task was impossible. By the time I arrived at Picture House, my transformation had struck me down midstride. I picked myself up and climbed onto Dusty's back.

The miniature city was glowing a faint orange, reflecting the last traces of the sunset.

Where would the pothunters have hidden the basket? I struggled to remember the night when all of this had started. After I'd thrown the blazing tumbleweed over the edge of the cliff, we'd waited on top. After a short while the flashlight of the pothunters had appeared below as they left in the direction of Enchanted Mesa. If they had stopped soon after to hide the artifacts, I would have noticed. They had kept going. They must have hidden the basket and the seed pot fairly close to Picture House, before I first saw the beam.

I made my best guess about the spot where that flashlight had first appeared. I intended to search from that spot back to Picture House. The basket and the pot should be hidden somewhere close to that route.

By the light of a quarter moon I started searching, but the rat's superior night vision didn't promise to be much help in this hopeless tangle of boulders and junipers, pinyons and oak brush, yucca and cactus and more boulders. The pot and the medicine bundle could be anywhere!

I scurried around and around, more desperate by the moment. What were my chances of coming across the basket!

I was sick with dread as I hurried my way toward the ruin, hoping against hope. Dusty was crisscrossing my path, nose down like a bloodhound. I realized she was my only hope. "Help me, Dusty!" I hollered. "Find that seed jar! This is the most important one ever! The basket will be with the pot! Find that pot, Dusty, please find it!"

We'd almost worked our way back to Picture House, and I was all in a panic when Dusty crawled underneath a slab in the rockfall that leaned back against the cliff close to the wall of pictures. When she came out, then stuck her nose back in, I knew Old Faithful had come through for me again.

I crawled in and found the seed jar there with its black-on-white lines, the one I was looking for. And here, next to it, was the basket.

I peered over the edge of the basket and looked in. The contents were gone! The stone pipe, the porcupine's teeth, the roots, and especially the pouches, all gone. In their place, small rocks and sticks! I rustled through them and found not even one pouch.

Packrats!

Suddenly I heard voices, and I darted out of there. I led Dusty to a hiding place close by. The bright light of a lantern was heading our way.

I shouldn't have been surprised. I'd know their voices anywhere. I hurried to the top of one of the big slabs where I could see.

The pothunters were kneeling, and the bearded one— Duke—was reaching under the slab where their plunder was hidden. "Still under here," he reported.

Their socks were showing through the holes in their boots. Beside them lay two shovels and a pick.

"Hey, look at this! Nothing but sticks and rocks!"

"Packrats!" Rodney cried. "Man, we are having nothing but rotten luck with packrats!"

"This basket is only a basket without all that medicine man's stuff!"

"I know! We've been ripped off by packrats!"

From far above, the owl called *hoo, hoo-hoo-hoo, hoo-oo, hoo-oo.*

The pothunters stood still as statues. Again came the call of the owl.

"Spooky," said Duke, who wasn't the one I remembered being superstitious.

"You know, Duke," said his brother, seeing his opportunity, "I just don't have a good feeling about digging tonight. We've had rotten luck here. . . . I still think we shouldn't have come back for the basket even if it is so valuable. We still have to get a tow truck! What if that kid saw something?"

Duke was pulling on his beard and looking around like he wanted to kill someone. "Shut up! That kid didn't see anything! Everything's too well hid and you know it!"

He looked around as if he were being watched, and now his eyes fixed on the dance plaza. A coyote stood in the open there, staring. It looked to me like the coyote was staring at me, not them. In the reflected light of the lantern, the coyote's eyes seemed ablaze.

Duke pulled his pistol and blasted away at the coyote, once, twice. The coyote just stood there. Duke paused to get another look. The coyote yawned, then walked away slowly out of the light.

"That was too strange," I heard Rodney say as I was hastening down the backside of the slab. I wanted to get down there fast and add to the confusion. I ran out into the open and bit one of them on the toes before he ever saw me coming, bit the other one before he could react, then bit the first one again. I had those guys jumping! Never did I expect the gun to go off, but that's what it did, with a colossal explosion that sent me leaping for cover.

"I've shot myself in the foot!" Duke roared. Then he screamed and cursed, and cursed some more, and screamed again.

From hiding, I watched his brother remove what was left of the tip of the boot, then tear strips from his shirt and improvise a bandage.

They left with Duke hopping on one leg, hanging onto his brother's side. They took only the flashlight, leaving behind the lantern, two shovels and a pick, the seed jar and the basket.

They weren't heading back to Enchanted Mesa and their dead truck. They were staggering toward Encantado, and they had an awful long way to go. Dusty and I watched their flashlight disappear as I realized what I had to do next.

I already knew where the closest nest was; I'd been partway in there before.

Behind the leaning stab I found the big mound of sticks, bones, and rocks. I had to find those pouches, no matter what. It was up to me.

It didn't matter if I was terrified. I was going in there, and I wasn't going to be run out. No matter what it took, I was going to find those pouches.

Inside, I threaded my way farther than I'd gone before. I found a nest, but it was abandoned. I continued through the barest of passages among the cactus spines. Then I heard drumming deep inside the maze. They could hear or smell me coming.

I came to a second nest. This one was lined with grasses and feathers. No sign of the pouches, but I didn't expect them here. They'd be in the food cache or in the midden.

In front of me a pair of eyes glowed, then a second pair and a third. The drumming was furious, deafening. I kept moving forward, out of the tunnel and into the next chamber where they awaited me.

They leapt on me, squeaking and clawing and gnashing. But I was on fire, and I fought back. I fought with tooth and claw and rage. I was fighting for my mother's life. Tumbling, scratching, clawing, biting, squeaking with fury, I fought them back.

More rats arrived. I don't know how many. White-hot, I fought them, too. Suddenly they backed off, all of them, looking at me with the fear of the unknown. I rushed them, bellowing with all my might, and they turned and ran.

I tried to calm myself and my thundering heart. Quickly I began sniffing and looking around. In a corner of the packrats' cache, on top of a pile of pinyon nuts, I found the small buckskin bundles, ten of them. I couldn't remember how many there had been. Did I have them all? I'd better investigate the rest of the rat runs, make sure I had them all.

In the trash dump, one of the rats I'd fought was waiting for me. I drummed furiously with a hind leg and the rat disappeared. No more pouches, but as I glanced around the walls, I noticed the set of porcupine teeth, and then a smooth piece of bone sticking out, just barely.

Eagle-wing bone.

The flute was wedged in there tight, but I pulled it free.

Eleven trips outside, and I had my prizes. Dusty sniffed them approvingly. Now to get all those pouches home . . . how were Dusty and I going to carry them? She'd never been one to carry things in her mouth, not even a stick. Maybe I could train her to carry the basket . . . there just wasn't time. I had to carry the basket myself. But for that I would need human hands.

The flute's the answer, I thought. I only needed to play a few certain notes on it, if only I could learn them. I hurried to the picture wall.

The bighorn sheep and the spirits, the bird-headed people and the bear tracks were gleaming in the moonlight. But they didn't hold the answer. Cricket had said the answer was in the spirals.

Here they were, in between the two Kokopellis: the two spirals side-by-side that had once reminded me of

157

the eyes of an owl. The spirals were the clue. How could the spirals possibly be the clue?

I saw nothing but two spirals ringed by corn.

The corn . . . the eyes of the owl . . .

The owl? I asked myself. Could that be it? The spirals contain the message, Cricket had said, and the spirals are the eyes of the owl!

I had to try. If ever I was going to try, it had to be now.

I held the flute sideways against my face, hoping to imitate the owl with the flute: *hoo, hoo-hoo-hoo, hoo-oo, hoo-oo!*

My first try produced nothing close to the correct rhythm. I kept trying, over and over again. At last I put the notes together in the right timing, producing the call of the nesting great horned owl of Picture House.

At that moment, I was myself again.

Dusty's eyes went huge.

I gathered up the pouches, placed them in the basket, snatched up the flute and the seed jar, and took off sprinting in the moonlight. We knew the way by heart.

Chapter Twenty

As my mother held tight to my hands, she craned her neck to see the ancient buckskin pouches I had brought. Her breathing was far worse. Standing at the big table, my father had his pocket knife out and was cutting the ancient yucca cords that bound them at their necks. Cricket was gently opening them up.

My mother started coughing and then gasping for breath. When that subsided, she laughed low and painfully and motioned me closer. I leaned close to hear what she would say.

"Like when you were in the incubator," she whispered.

"Fight for every breath," I encouraged her.

"This one!" Cricket cried, and I hurried to the table. He was pointing to the dried and perfectly preserved leaves of a plant I'd never seen before, rolled tightly around each other.

"Boil a little water," Cricket said. "We'll make some tea."

I returned to my mother's side, where her hand rested on Dusty's head.

"Don't worry," I told her. "Cricket's found the right one."

"Good," she whispered. "I want to try this ancient medicine."

I was dead tired but I made myself promise I wouldn't go to sleep. My mother took a cup of tea when it was ready, and then she waited a while, and then she took another cup.

I looked around and Cricket was gone, but shortly thereafter the music of the flute filled the room. My father looked around, mystified. This time all three of us were hearing it. My dad didn't speak, other than through his eyes, which were suddenly filled with hope.

I looked atop the bookcase. The bright green insect was playing his flute, wings raised and vibrating faster than the eye could see.

The flute played on through the night. The rattling in my mother's chest gradually subsided, and she wheezed for breath less often. We sat with her as she fell asleep. As the first hint of dawn was showing outside, she woke. My father gave her a third cup of the ancient remedy, and she drank it readily. Her fever had broken. Her breathing, though ragged, had improved.

"What happened to the music?" my mother wondered, and then we noticed that the notes of the flute had died out like a wind subsiding, so gently we hadn't noticed its passing.

In the blinding light of the sunrise, I thought I saw someone in the field. "It's Cricket," my father said, and when I looked again, I glimpsed the old man walking away with his gunnysack over his back, disappearing into the corn.

My mother sat up in bed. "I'm going to be okay," she said. "I want to see Cricket. I'm afraid he's leaving."

"He's already gone," I told her.

"Run and see if you can find him, Tep. I want to thank him."

Dusty at my side, I made my way through our fields and toward the sunrise. On all sides, the rarest food crops in the Americas were growing in a riot of leaf, tendril, and flower. I thought I heard a few notes from the flute. I paused and strained to catch them. The flute was faint, yet unmistakable: it spoke of the wind and rippling water, the stars, the wings of birds, seeds sprouting, plants growing, life renewing endlessly.

My hopes soared that I at least might say good-bye. I did catch one more glimpse. I saw Kokopelli's silhouette, playing the flute, as he disappeared into the rising sun.

I made my way toward my patch of Picture House

corn, hoping he'd visited there and given it his special attention. I had a feeling I wouldn't find bare ground.

Every last kernel had germinated. Those first leafy shoots were waving green as can be in a sudden gust of wind blowing back toward the south. I went back into the cabin, and I told them Cricket was gone. I also told them about the Picture House corn.

"Well, I'll be a Manure Specialist!" my father declared.

"And I'll be the boss," I reminded him.

My father stayed close to my mother. I visited her study in the basement. There was something I wanted to look up. I found a section on the flute player in *Rock Art of the Great Southwest:*

When the human beings came into this world, through a hole in the sky of the previous one, they were accompanied by two insect people.

Two of them, I thought.

These were two special insect people, special beings with great powers and extraordinary courage. Shortly after the human beings had emerged into this world, they were climbing a mountain, and when they reached the top they met a great bird, an eagle. One of the insect people, acting as a spokesman, asked the eagle for permission to live

162

in this world. The eagle answered that it might be possible, but first they must be tested.

The eagle held two arrows. "Step closer," he told the insect people, and the two did so. "Keep your eyes open as I pierce them," the eagle ordered, and he stabbed with great force, stopping the arrow points at the last instant. The two insect people, on behalf of the human beings, did not blink.

"I can see you are people of substance," the eagle observed. "But the final test is much more difficult, and you will not pass it, I believe."

"We are ready," replied the two. At this, the eagle produced a bow, and shot the first through with an arrow. The insect person produced his flute and played a beautiful song, as if the arrow were not sticking through his body and out the other side.

"So," said the eagle, "you are people with power, that is plain to see." At this, he shot the second through, and now both played beautifully on their flutes, so beautifully that their bodies were healed with the magic power of their song.

The eagle now gave permission for the human beings to occupy this world.

I returned the book to its place on my mother's bookshelf. And then I used her telephone. I made two calls, one to the BLM ranger and one to the sheriff. I told them that the Bishop brothers were headed toward Encantado, and I told them where to find their truck and the artifacts nearby. I also told them that we had the seed jar and the medicine bundle.

But I didn't tell them about the flute. I couldn't tell anyone about the flute. Someone would surely blow on it, as I had.

The summer advanced with hot days and little rain. My mother's health returned and she set to work summarizing the results of her research. As boss of the farm for the rest of the season, I was making sure our crops were especially well fertilized.

Sometimes at night, lying awake, I'd find myself missing my adventures, remembering almost with fondness my furry body and my handsome, bushy tail. What I missed most was riding bareback on Dusty, the wind in my whiskers. But I didn't miss any of it enough to want to try that flute again. Packrats live a risky life and that's for sure.

Our crops were going to far outproduce our best previous year. We would have our hands full when the time came for threshing, sifting, winnowing, and drying all those seeds. They would include the seeds of a new sweet gourd. In a few years we'd have enough to offer them through our catalog.

My father would often remark, as he watched the

ravens flying low across our fields, how strange it was that they seemed to have quit raiding us.

Coyote, too, never stole another ear of corn or nipped another melon.

The flute remains well hidden, under a false bottom in one of my collections of fossil seashells.

Dusty keeps my secret. We wait for Cricket's return.

DON'T MISS ANY OF THE STORIES BY AWARD-WINNING AUTHOR AVI

Available in Bookstores Everywhere
or See Below for Ordering Information

☐ AMANDA JOINS THE CIRCUS   80338-0/$3.99 US/$4.99 Can

☐ KEEP YOUR EYE ON AMANDA!   80337-2/$3.99 US/$4.99 Can

☐ THE BARN   72562-2/$4.99 US/$6.99 Can

☐ BLUE HERON   72043-4/$4.50 US/$6.50 Can

☐ THE MAN WHO WAS POE   73022-7/$4.99 US/$6.50 Can

☐ POPPY   72769-2/$4.99 US/$6.99 Can

☐ POPPY AND RYE   79717-8/$4.99 US/$6.99 Can

☐ PUNCH WITH JUDY   72980-6/$4.50 US/$5.99 Can

☐ ROMEO AND JULIET TOGETHER
(AND ALIVE!) AT LAST   70525-7/$4.50 US/$5.99 Can

☐ S.O.R. LOSERS   69993-1/$4.50 US/$5.99 Can

☐ SOMETHING UPSTAIRS   79086-6/$4.99 US/$6.50 Can

☐ THE TRUE CONFESSIONS OF
CHARLOTTE DOYLE   72885-0/$4.99 US/$6.99 Can

☐ "WHO WAS THAT MASKED
MAN, ANYWAY?"   72113-0/$3.99 US/$4.99 Can

☐ WINDCATCHER   71805-7/$4.99 US/$6.99 Can